FATAL TURN

BOOK 13 IN THE DI GILES SERIES

ANNA-MARIE MORGAN

ALSO BY ANNA-MARIE MORGAN

For Jean, with love

1

FATAL HIKE

Mark Turner hitched his rucksack higher, relishing the breeze which cooled the wet patch on the back of his denim shirt and feathered his cheek.

Hat up, he dried his brow with the back of a hand, narrowing amber eyes against the horizon. The yellows and greens of the hills in the foreground paled to grey-blue and purple in the distance. Tall sentinels comprising the growing Mid-Wales turbine army were mere centimetres high on the skyline as they gently spun in the breeze, generating electricity for a myriad anonymous homes. Above them, a sheet of fine cloud covering the sky began dissipating in the sun's glare.

The three hours since leaving home had led to a gnawing in his stomach. Perhaps he would stop. Perhaps he wouldn't. He didn't always. There was an odd satisfaction in going the whole day without sustenance. Kept the body lean and the mind sharp.

At thirty-three, he had walked these hills and moors

many times, pushing himself harder and further. But not today.

Today, he had one goal in mind — to find the cave he had come across, by accident, two weeks before.

The entrance was small, barely enough for a man to squeeze in sideways, but he could see that it opened up somewhat inside.

He hadn't entered on the previous occasion, prevented by a tremor throughout his core, sweat on his forehead, and an unusual thicket of fear as icy water invaded his hair, and he surveyed the dank, dark beyond.

This time, equipped with head torch, rope, pocket knife, and determination, he would enter and conquer it. The cave would be his. He would leave his unmistakable mark, like Edmundson, planting his Norwegian flag before the ill-fated Scott arrived. That would silence the dissenters — the doubters on Facebook and Twitter.

HE WAITED, taut as stretched canvas, in the shadows.

He could hear the man outside. Could hear him breathing. Almost.

Any moment now, Turner would encroach, unaware of the danger lurking inside this dark, foul-smelling orifice.

Water dripped from the roots hanging through the ceiling. The same element that had carved this niche in the rock over eons. It chilled the air, lying in small, yellowing pools at his feet. Like urine. Some of it was urine. He had relieved himself, not five minutes before. No requirement for niceties here. He could do what he liked. And would.

Turner set himself up. He shared too much. They all did. Pouring their lives onto social media like milk onto cereal, not caring where the splashes ended up. It was fuel for him. And for the notebook he copied it into, noting times and dates whenever and wherever they appeared. They laid the path for him to tread.

Funny, he didn't feel nervous. Instead, a quiet confidence had him standing tall, shoulders wide, feet planted firmly. It would be quick. His mother said he had muscular hands. Said he was born with them. That, and hair on the sides of his face and forehead. The facial hair had long since gone. But the powerful hands remained. Strong. Deadly.

Seconds ticked. What was he doing out there? Checking his equipment? Was he singing to himself? What tune was that? He couldn't quite get it. Perhaps he would enquire before he choked all life from the singer.

MARK SWITCHED ON HIS TORCH, scanning through the opening. Above him, roots like distorted fingers reached into the semi-darkness from rock, discoloured by salts. His every movement echoed off the walls.

Twelve feet beyond, he could see a narrow cleft, possibly a passage. He paused, hand resting on the knife clipped to his belt. The gut-wrenching tremor was back. Something wasn't right.

He pulled out his mobile phone, activating the camera, enabling him to gather the proof needed to silence his social media critics. He had filmed the opening. Now he laboured on the inside, so experienced cavers would know the cavern was genuine and not one they had ever seen before. He didn't understand their need to argue with him about his discovery, questioning whether he had been drinking or out in the sun too long, using violent language.

The discovery of the cave was not the issue. They had

taken exception to his visceral reaction to it. They doubted the tremulous fear, thinking he was exaggerating or, at least, embellishing.

The fact they did not know him was, to his mind anyway, no excuse. His reaction? An increased determination to shove the proof down their throats. Let them come and feel it for themselves.

He had his back to the unexplored fissure at the opposite end of the cave, busy filming the outside, through the entrance, when the garrotte came over his head and around his neck.

Fingers and nails vainly tore at the wire, scratching his own skin as it bled, the wire cutting deeper and deeper, breathing increasingly impossible until he felt his legs and bladder go.

The killer let Mark Turner's lifeless body fall to the floor.

MISSING

"Good morning, ma'am." Sergeant Dewi Hughes grinned at her. "How's the head?"

Yvonne pulled a face and straightened her crumpled skirt, aware he was referring to her getting more than a little merry at Callum's summer barbecue, and singing 'I Will Survive' at the top of her lungs with Dai and Tasha as backing singers.

"It was the Daiquiri that did it." She brushed her forehead. "I'm still feeling delicate."

Dewi laughed, hand to his belly. "It was good to see you let your hair down for a change, ma'am." He handed her a coffee the colour of chocolate. "There you go, get that down you. Help clear the cobwebs."

The DI smiled. "I'm sure the coffee will pep me up." She nodded at the file in Dewi's hands. "What have you got for me?"

Dewi's face sobered. "Missing person, ma'am, Mark Turner. No-one has heard from him in over a week. He didn't show up for work and his sister said they had planned to meet last Wednesday for lunch, but he didn't go. Uniform carried out a welfare check at his home, and no sign of him. His wallet and phone were absent, but he doesn't appear to have packed a bag or taken any clothing with him."

Yvonne frowned. "Maybe he changed his mind about meeting his sister and didn't fancy work this week?"

Dewi checked his notes. "The sister said this is highly unusual for her brother. They are close and she said he has never cancelled without calling her and letting her know."

"Okay." Yvonne pursed her lips. "Can I see what you've got?"

Dewi handed it over.

"So, he's a hiker?"

"He is. He's been at it for many years. Lots of experience. His sister believes he may have had an accident on one of his hikes, and may be lying in a field somewhere."

The DI nodded. "We'd better get Search and Rescue involved. Did he have a hike scheduled for last week? Do we know?"

"Lisa Turner, that's his sister, said he'd been talking about a cave he discovered on a previous hike up on the Dolfor Moors. He posted about it on social media, apparently."

"Okay, well, let's look at that, shall we? If we are involving search teams, we had better have an idea where they should look."

"Right you are, ma'am. I asked Callum to bring up his Facebook, YouTube, and Twitter profiles. He should have done that by now."

Yvonne finished her coffee, wincing at the bitterness, and followed her sergeant over to where Callum was pouring over social media.

The DC ran his hands through his hair. "Looks like things were getting heavy on his profile pages, ma'am."

"What do you mean?" Yvonne frowned.

"People doubting things he was saying about a cave he told them he'd discovered."

"Why? What was he saying?"

"That the cave had an unusual energy about it. Claimed that when he approached it, he felt afraid. Like it had strange powers. He said it made his body shake."

The DI rubbed her chin. "Some cave."

"Quite."

"So, why was it getting heated? Why were people arguing with him about it?"

Callum shrugged. "I don't think it started out that way. Looks like it began with people questioning why the cave made him afraid, and it escalated from there. He had more supporters than detractors, but those with objections were pretty vehement about it. And Turner appears to have been sensitive to the comments."

"And yet, as a seasoned hiker, he will have come across places like that cave previously, surely? Why did this one make him afraid?"

Callum leaned back in his chair. "God knows, ma'am, but he told them he would get video evidence of its existence, and get GPS coordinates so they could see for themselves."

"Okay, well..." Yvonne peered over Callum's shoulder. "Do we know where this cave is? If we set up a search for him, that is the obvious place to start."

"That's the problem." Callum scratched his head. "We know he found it on a Dolfor Moors hike. What we don't know is where. As you know, it covers a sizeable area. The mouth of the cave cannot be that obvious, or others would have discovered it before. It could take some time to locate it and an impressive amount of manpower."

"What about the photos? Can we tell from them?"

Her DC shook his head. "I'm afraid not, ma'am. He didn't photograph it at all on the first trip."

"Well, what about cavers? Can they help us find it?"

Callum nodded. "We can ask them, though it appears from the comments as though many of them were pretty sceptical. No-one has ever written about it."

"They might know the geology well enough to give us pointers for a likely search area?" Yvonne placed her hands on her hips with a sigh. "It doesn't sound like this will be a simple task. Get onto his sister, Lisa. Ask her if she knows the route he normally took on his hikes. We can get an idea from that, at least. Give the search teams a fighting chance. They can get helicopter over the area, in any event. She could be right. He could be in a field somewhere."

"I'll get on to the sister." Callum nodded.

YVONNE WAS glad of her light-cotton, sleeveless blouse. The day had started hot. Even at seven o'clock that morning, the temperature on the gauge in her car read eighteen centi-grade. Now it had to be at least ten-to-twelve degrees hotter than that.

The whirring of helicopter blades, slicing the air over-head, accompanied the distant sound of approaching sirens, and the chatter of medical and police personnel.

Yvonne approached the half-acre cordon set up by uniform in a field on the moors, off a narrow dirt-track road that ran along the top, between Dolfor village and the village of Llanbadarn Fynydd.

They had found Mark Turner in a crumpled heap in the field, having had the life garrotted from him.

That someone had murdered him was obvious. What was not obvious was where that killing occurred, whether in the same field or elsewhere?

The DI pulled her mask down over her nose and mouth and crouched close to the body, her plastic suit crackling.

The killer had fashioned the garrotte from cheese wire; improving the grip with duct tape around the plastic handles.

The wire embedded in the victim's throat. His eyes, open and bulging, had dried in the heat. Yvonne swallowed the lump in her throat, her abdomen tightening as she suppressed a gag.

That he had fought for his life was clear from the deep scratches on his throat where he had tried to get a purchase on the wire biting into his neck. It was all too easy to visualise that desperate struggle.

She cast her eyes around. The landscape was breathtakingly open. The DI could understand the thrill that must accompany a day-long hike. Without official personnel strewn across the area, there was only sheep and birds for company. That, and the modern windmills, barely moving in the distance.

If she could draw any consolation from events, it was that Mark Turner had died doing what loved in a place he enjoyed exploring. That would be some comfort to his family and friends.

She thought of his sister and how the news would turn everything she knew on its head.

Yvonne pressed her lips tight together, standing. It was their turn, now. Her team would catch this killer. Mark would have justice.

Dewi approached her from the road.

"Grim." He sighed. "That must have taken some doing, a

fit adult male like that. It would need immense strength."

She nodded. "Most likely approached from behind. Once the garrotte was in place, young and fit or not, he would have had one hell of a battle to remove it. Element of surprise, and all that."

Her sergeant nodded. "Do you think they killed him here?"

She shook her head. "It's possible, but that would assume he knew his killer well enough to allow him close, and to approach from behind. It's too open. I would lay money on him having died elsewhere, somewhere a killer could approach unseen and unheard, even if they knew each other." She nodded towards the SOCO personnel. "We'll see whether they find tracks. I think it likely they dumped him from a four-by-four. It will have left the road somewhere up there." She pointed above them, before turning back to examine the hard earth and grass, grazed to mere centimetres in height by sheep. "I think these may be the tracks. May not get a tread from them, but I suspect they threw the body from a vehicle."

"Shall I set up a meeting with his sister?" Dewi checked his watch. "Time's moving on. It's just after eleven."

She nodded. "Arrange one for as soon as she feels able to talk to us, Dewi. I'll speak to Dai and Callum. We will need rather a lot of social media trawling to trace all the contacts he has had over the past couple of months. I'd lay bets on his killer being one of them."

"Yes, you may be right."

The DI stepped back, allowing SOCO to continue their vital work. Not until she got back to the car did she disrobe from the hazmat. In the distance, the windmills were silent. Not enough breeze. Just like Mark, they had ceased breathing.

3

A LIFE LIVED

Lisa Turner was tiny. Not much taller than five foot, Yvonne guessed. Her shoulder-length, straw-blonde hair held back in a loose ponytail, she wore a grass-green summer dress, dotted with petite white flowers, and sandals.

She appeared lost, like her mind was awash with the whys and wherefores. Aware of her surroundings, but not involved in them. Still trying to unravel what had gone wrong, and why she had not been able to prevent it.

The DI understood. Had been there. Only time could drive away pain like that. Mere words were not powerful enough, however comforting others intended them to be.

Yvonne knew the importance of silence at such a moment. She gave the younger woman ample space, sitting quietly until Lisa was ready to talk.

"I knew," Lisa began, running her fingers over swollen eyes, drying infinite tears, lifting the back of her hand to her nose. "Something bad had happened to him, it was obvious. He would have let me know. He would have called me."

"Of course."

"He didn't have a chance, did he?"

"No, I don't think he did."

"What can I do to help?" Lisa looked at the DI, her red eyes open, questioning, soulful.

"One thing we need is the route he would have taken on his hike. Do you have any idea what that would have been?"

Lisa nodded. "He kept all of his maps in a box under his bed. He didn't need to use the local ones much anymore, but he would have marked out the route the first time he used it and, again, if he deviated from it. It'll be in that box, guaranteed."

Yvonne made a note. "Thank you."

Lisa sighed. "You're welcome. I guess I will have to sort through his things. I don't think I can get my head around that at the moment."

Yvonne shook hers. "You won't have to worry about that. Not yet, anyway. Our forensics team will be there a while, yet. In fact, it could be a week or two before you can have access."

"Of course." Lisa rose from her seat. "I'm fetching water. Would you like some?"

The DI held up a hand. "You go ahead. I am all right, thank you."

With Mark's sister gone, Yvonne cast her eyes around the lounge of the town flat. It showed a vibrant, modern taste. The colours of the lime sofa and pink rug, popped. The shelving and coffee table were square and chunky. Photographs dotted around were of youngsters laughing and having a pleasurable time. Mark Turner's sister was someone with a busy social calendar.

When she returned, Lisa set her glass down on the coffee table in front of them.

Yvonne continued the interview. "Did your brother

mention to you anyone he had concerns about, or was afraid of? Someone who might do him harm?"

The woman tilted her head, taking several seconds to think about it. "He talked about bullying on social media, but it was a general sort of thing. He didn't mention anybody in particular, only said he sometimes felt that people argued for the sake of it. Trolling, you know. He said it was hard for him to have a serious conversation. He received death threats, too."

"Death threats?" Yvonne's eyes widened. "From whom?"

"He didn't say."

"Did he say what form these threats took? Were they verbal? On social media?"

Lisa shook her head. "I don't know, I'm afraid. He said it was about a cave he'd discovered. He didn't give me any more details. I asked, but something distracted him. Said he'd fill me in later, but he didn't get around to it. He didn't seem that bothered. I got the impression he thought the entire thing pathetic. He disagreed with others on social media often."

The DI nodded. "I think many people have been there. It's easy for someone to be obnoxious from an armchair, but he didn't mention anyone out to harm him? Or anyone he had concerns about?"

"No, I'm afraid he didn't." Lisa sipped her water. "I'd have remembered if he had. I meant to ask him again, but hadn't had the opportunity."

"Of course." Yvonne pressed her lips together. "Do you have any other family around here?" she asked. "Any more brothers or sisters? Parents?"

Lisa shook her head. "It was just myself and Mark. Mum died when we were little and dad passed away after a heart attack, three years ago."

"Oh, I am sorry." The DI's gaze was heavy with gravitas, as she studied Lisa's face. "So much tragedy."

The younger woman pulled back. "I'm okay, don't feel sorry for me. You have a killer to find. My brother's killer. Don't waste any of your energy on me. I'll be all right. But, if I can help in this investigation, please let me know. Mark deserves no less from us."

Yvonne nodded. "You're right, and I promise you we will leave no stone unturned in this inquiry."

"Thank you." Lisa's smile did not reach her eyes. "I believe you won't."

CID CLATTERED WITH ACTIVITY, the murder investigation team was in full flow.

Yvonne took a moment to study her team as they focussed on their tasks. She was proud of them. Every one of her officers poured their heart and soul into these investigations. Late nights, sleepless ones, they had known many together. That was the unseen, often untold, part of public service. The stuff they did for the good of others, the excess overtime, losing those precious hours with friends and families. The extra pay didn't nearly cover the true cost, but they did it for love of their fellow humans, and for their need to get justice for the victims, and do what was right. And she knew they would do it again, whenever necessary, on this inquiry. Yes, she was as proud of her team as a new mother of her baby.

Callum and Dai had delved into Mark Turner's social media, gathering names and details of those who had interacted with him in any significant way, paying particular attention to those who had argued with him over his claims, and those who had given positive feedback.

Dewi listed close friends and contacts in Mark's personal life, particularly any who were aware of his hiking routes.

Yvonne wanted the information in time for her next briefing, where they could review it together with the first of the SOCO and pathology reports.

She approached the two DCs.

Her voice behind them made Callum jump. "Ma'am," he said, straightening.

"How are you doing?" She eyed Mark Turner's Facebook page on their screen.

"It really had become heated, the discussion about the cave which Mark alleged he'd found." Callum tossed his pen onto the desk.

"In what way? What was the argument?"

Callum pointed to the relevant comments. "Looks like Mark could not remember the exact co-ordinates of the cave. He wasn't a fan of GPS. He preferred to free-wheel it, by the look of things. He even went without food for most of the day, to push himself harder. So, when he found the cave, he only had his memory to go on. I get the impression that he didn't think he would go back there again. It made him uncomfortable. It was only afterwards, during the discussions with others, he appeared to change his mind. Then, he wanted to find it, to prove to the doubters that what he was saying was true."

"So, his arm was twisted, in effect?" The DI frowned.

Dai checked his notes. "I would agree with Callum, I think these comments motivated him to go back."

Yvonne nodded. "Okay. So, who was he talking to?"

Callum rubbed his stubble. "I've noted the principal players." He handed her a sheet of paper.

"And I'll print off the notable comments for you, see what you think."

"How many people were getting angry in the argument?"

"Four, altogether, three of whom are hikers. One of them is also a potholer."

"Did any issue threats? Threaten to kill him?"

Callum shook his head. "Not that I have seen. Why?"

Yvonne sighed. "Oh, it's just something his sister said to me. He told her he had received a death threat, but didn't offer further details."

Callum scratched his head. "Well, I'll keep an eye out. We are hoping to have access to his personal messages later today or tomorrow. There could be something in those."

"I see." The DI nodded. "Excellent work. Keep going. I want the names and details of all those involved in that discussion."

"Will do. I'll get on with printing off the post and all the comments. I'll do the same for Turner's YouTube video."

"Great. At the very least, we can talk to the key players about this discussion. See what comes out of that."

MARK TURNER'S YouTube videos documented his various walks through the Welsh countryside, of which there were many. He appeared to have built up a sizeable following, comprising several hundred individuals.

Two weeks before his fatal hike, Mark had posted a video of himself walking a route which the detectives had found marked on a map in the box under his bed.

In the video, he stated his intention to explore the mysterious cave he had discovered on a walk ten days prior.

He had filmed the video in ten-minute bursts, high-lighting things that grabbed his eye, such as wildlife, or interesting features of the landscape.

Yvonne was taken with the thirty-two-year-old's enthusiasm. His eyes shone as he explained what he was doing or seeing.

Her gut wrenched at the knowledge that a vicious killer had extinguished that light.

At least, they now knew the primary route he had taken on the fatal day. What they didn't know, however, was the deviation he would have taken to get to the cave. This was because Mark, in his YouTube video, had failed to locate the entrance.

The DI pulled at her bottom lip as she pondered this. Mark's video camera was not with his body, nor at his flat. It was possible, if not likely, the killer had taken it. Mark may have captured something at the time of his death, the killer would not have risked leaving it behind.

"What route are we going with?" Dewi asked as he passed her a mug of tea.

"Well, I think we ask the search teams to follow the map and video and we'll get the help of local geologists to pinpoint the likeliest places for the cave to be. Widen the search according to their advice. I have a hunch the killer found the cave, or knew of it, and waited there for Mark to turn up. If we find the cave, we may have the murder scene. Regardless, someone killed Mark on that hike, and we need to know where."

Dewi nodded. "He was a busy man."

"What do you mean?" The DI sipped on her tea.

"He worked full time as a security guard at a local super-market, and had signed up as a volunteer fireman, intending to change careers and become a full-time firefighter."

"Really?" Yvonne narrowed her eyes. "Amazing. I was only marvelling earlier at the amount of energy he must have to complete these hikes and make his videos. Then, I find out he had two careers."

Dewi nodded. "A remarkable man."

"Very much so. Can you get on to the supermarket, Dewi, and find out if he had had any run-ins with anyone in his work, any recent incidents."

"Will do."

The DI's gaze became unfocussed. "What a waste, Dewi. What a damn waste of a man's life."

4

WHISPERINGS

Rob Tanner was a thirty-seven-year-old shop manager in Newtown. The store, J.J. Martin and Sons, sold camping and hiking gear.

He agreed to see Yvonne at the shop during his lunch break, telling her he had around twenty minutes.

The DI climbed the steps, opening the door. The bell chimed in her ear.

A blonde-haired, handsome male with large biceps stepped from behind the counter. He approached, eyeing her with a steady gaze. There was a stiffness in his gait and he wasn't smiling.

The DI extended her hand, anyway. "Yvonne Giles. I'm here to see Robert Tanner."

He gave it a firm shake. "That will be me." Tanner had to be around six feet in height.

Yvonne felt tiny in comparison. "I understand you are the manager here?"

He nodded. "Yes, I am. Listen, do you mind? I just need to lock the door."

Yvonne moved back to allow him access. "Of course. I

am hoping not to keep you too long." She flicked her eyes around the store. They had stacked a lot of stuff in a compact space. The room couldn't have been much more than fifteen square feet.

"It's okay," He said, drawing the bolt across. "We close for thirty minutes at lunchtime, anyway."

Yvonne nodded. "That should be time enough."

"So, how may I help?" Rob pulled out a chair and stool from behind the counter, offering the former to the DI.

"Thank you." She sat, waiting for him to join her.

His bottom overhung the tiny stool.

The DI mused that it had to be uncomfortable, and thought about offering a swap for the chair, but he began talking and she forgot about it.

"You wanted to speak to me about Mark Turner?" he asked, grabbing foil-wrapped sandwiches from a backpack. "Do you mind?"

She shook her head. "You eat. Don't worry about me. I am happy."

"Would you like one?" He held the open packet towards her. "Cheese and onion, made by Helen, my partner."

The DI held up a hand. "No, thank you, it's kind of you to offer, but I have an egg roll waiting for me back at the office."

He took a bite of the sandwich.

"I assume you have heard about Mark's untimely death. I understand you knew him."

Rob rocked his head from side-to-side. "I wouldn't say I knew him that well. He'd been in to the shop once or twice for items of hiking gear. I think he bought crampons, one time, maybe a jacket or two. We exchanged a few words, only that really. I was sorry to hear about his death. He was too young to die."

Yvonne nodded, tilting her head, eyes narrowing. "Someone murdered him." She studied Tanner's face.

Rob continued chewing, saying nothing.

"I understand you commented on a recent Facebook post of his? A post regarding a cave he said he had found."

Rob paused mid-chew and swallowed. "I remember." He grunted, clearing his throat.

"You weren't convinced about his discovery." She knew that was an understatement. Rob Tanner had been obnoxious."

He set his sandwiches down. "Look, several of us have hiked out that way a few times and never come across any cave. No-one seems to have heard of it." He sighed. "But it wasn't so much that as the other stuff he mentioned."

"Other stuff?" The DI tilted her head.

"Yeah... All that stuff about feeling vibrations coming from it. I mean, what was all that about? He hadn't mentioned vibrations the first time he told the story. They came later. Further along in the comments. I got the impression he was enjoying the attention and was adding stuff on. I was sceptical, I mean, who has ever heard of a cave giving off vibrations? Really?"

"Perhaps, it was some sort of earth tremor?" Yvonne pressed her lips together.

Rob shook his head. "The British Geological Survey Seismology Team would catch anything of that sort, and they registered nothing in that area on the day Mark said he was there."

"Could he have gotten mixed up about the day?"

Rob shrugged. "He seemed pretty sure of the date. I mean, he didn't give a rough date. He was pretty exact."

"Perhaps something else caused the vibrations."

He pulled a face. "Mark said the cave made him vibrate.

That he felt tremors in his body. It just seemed to get more and more fantastical to me."

"So, you became angry and frustrated?"

"Well, yeah, I suppose I got frustrated, and that may have come across in my words."

"At one point, you told him to eff-off."

"Er, yeah, I did. He told me I didn't know the area as well as I thought. That annoyed me. I've been at this hiking business a long time. More than he had."

"Do you know where the cave is located, Rob?"

He shook his head. "He didn't give the location, funny that. I haven't come across any myself in that area, and I don't know any other hikers who have."

"Did you see Mark at all, after that exchange on social media?"

"No, not at all. He didn't come into the shop and, other than that, we wouldn't have bumped into each other. I don't live in town. I live in Welshpool and don't come into Newtown, aside from work, and I have never seen him in Welshpool."

"Right."

"I had nothing to do with his death, if that's what you think."

Yvonne pursed her lips. "I didn't say you did, but we will speak to everybody who knew him or had exchanges with him."

"Do you believe they murdered him because of that cave?"

Yvonne shrugged. "I don't know."

"But you think it's somehow involved?"

She nodded. "Anything is possible. How long have you been the manager of this store?"

He tilted his head, his eyes half-lidded. "Er... coming up

to ten years, now. I studied retail and business management in college. I got involved in hiking whilst I was studying."

"Do you enjoy it?"

He nodded. "I do. There isn't much I don't know about hiking, camping and climbing tackle."

"Is business good?"

"We get by. This is a popular destination for outdoor pursuits."

"I can imagine." She smiled, but her eyes continued to study his face.

Tanner checked his watch. "I must open again in five minutes."

Yvonne rose. "I'll let you get on." She passed him a card. "Contact me if you hear, or think of, anything else you feel relevant to our inquiry."

"Of course." He stood to see her to the door. "I am sorry that Mark is dead."

She shouldered her bag. "Thank you for your time."

Yvonne only needed walk a few minutes from the police station, to interview Daniel McCready,

Latham Park was Newtown's football stadium. The team performed well in the Welsh league, but the DI had never watched a single game. Perhaps she might take Tasha to see one sometime. Do something different.

She was still pondering this as she walked through the doors of the club and into the main hall; the venue used for events such as after-wedding parties, birthday parties, and so on.

Daniel, a travelling DJ, was at one end of the hall, setting up equipment. Two large speakers on stands, amplifiers, record decks, mixers, and jack leads. Paraphernalia everywhere.

He focussed on what he was doing, appearing not to notice the DI approach.

She cleared her throat, exaggerating the sound.

He looked up, his eyes narrowing.

"DI Giles. I'm here to speak with Daniel McCready."

"Aye, you're looking at him."

He was taller than she. Perhaps five-eleven. Wiry with sinewy arms. For all his lightness in stature, he lifted the heavy speakers without breaking sweat. His black hair had a short back and sides.

"Is now an awful time?" She paused, one hand holding her shoulder bag.

"Now is as good a time as any." He continued working. "I will check the sound after this. You won't be able to hear yourself think, let alone talk." He grinned and turned to her. "I don't mean to be rude. There's always so much to do."

She nodded. "I'm sorry to have to interrupt."

"No problem." He shouldered a rolled up jack lead. "You wanted to talk to me about Mark Turner?"

"Yes." She placed her bag on the floor, taking out a notebook and iPad. "I understand you knew him?"

"I did. I've known Mark since high school. We were never friends, but we both had an interest in hiking. I'm more of a rock climber, really, but I enjoy the occasional cross-country walk. We have been at the same meets, on times, but not recently."

"Sure. When was the last time you spoke to him?"

He stopped what he was doing, one hand on his hip, lips pursed. "Hmm... three weeks ago, maybe? Something like that."

"And how was he, then?"

He shrugged. "He was his usual self, as far as I could tell."

"Where was this?"

"What? Where I saw him?"

"Yes."

"A pub in town, I think. Might have been the Elephant." He continued plugging leads into equipment,.

Yvonne knew he meant the Elephant and Castle at the top of town. "A few weeks ago, you commented on a Facebook post of his. Do you remember that?"

He paused, turning to her. "I comment on lots of posts. I don't remember all of them. You'd have to remind me."

"If I tell you the post concerned a cave Mark believed he had found."

He tutted, flicking back his head. "Oh, that. What can I say? Believed is the operative word."

"What do you mean?"

"Well, he said he found it, and got vibrations from it, but he couldn't remember where this cave was and the few people who have tried to locate it since, have failed."

"Who tried to locate it."

"I don't know. I can't remember the names of everybody who commented. I just know that there were people who had been up in the area and failed to find it."

"So, you are telling me you didn't believe Mark's story."

"Look, even if he found a cave in that area, I think it's a bit of a stretch to believe that it made his entire body shake uncontrollably."

"Perhaps something about it scared him? The fear caused him to shake."

"Look, the man was a seasoned hiker. He'd been all over the place. I find it hard to accept that he was afraid of exploring the opening of a cave. Something about his story just didn't add up. It made no sense."

The DI grimaced. "Have you never experienced instinctive feeling about something? A sense of foreboding?"

"No." He continued sorting his equipment.

"You threw a drink over him, didn't you?"

"What?" She had his attention.

"Some comments on his post referred to your having thrown a beer at him. You were involved in that discussion. You ought to know what I mean."

He sighed, running his fingers through his hair. "You're right. I did throw a beer over him. We were both a little worse for wear and ran into each other on a pub crawl. It was a mate's birthday. Our two groups of friends were in the same pub. The Buck, I think. I don't know how it happened, but we ended up in a row about that bloody cave. I let my frustration get the better of me. I wouldn't usually. I rely on these pubs for my bread and butter. I get a lot of gigs in them with the decks, you know. The last thing I need is to get thrown out."

"And were you?"

"Was I what?"

"Thrown out?"

"No. Security came and spoke with us. Told us to calm down or they would eject us. We left each other alone after that."

"Why did you row?"

"He was talking about the cave really loudly, laughing about the comments he had had. I felt like he was doing it to get me riled. And I bit the bait. I couldn't help myself after a few drinks, you know? It's what lads are like when they get together and have a few. Things can get out of hand. Hell, I didn't go out intending to fight with him. He isn't..." He sighed. "He wasn't worth it. And I am not saying that as a reflection of my feelings on his death."

"You heard, then?"

"Of course I heard. I don't know anyone who hasn't. And, obviously, I wouldn't have wished him murdered. I wouldn't have wanted that. But that doesn't mean that I didn't find him irritating."

"They killed him with a garrotte."

"I know, and it's horrible, but I threw a drink over him. I didn't murder him."

"Where were you on Saturday?"

"Oh, I see. Like that is it?"

"Well?"

"I had a late gig in the Lion on that night."

"That was the evening. What were you doing in the day?"

He shrugged. "I was home prepping for the gig. From six pm, I was at the pub setting up my gear."

"And there are people who can vouch for your presence at home during the day?"

"Not really. I live on my own. I have a flat on Vaynor. Maybe a neighbour saw me around, but I doubt it. I didn't see a soul all day. I was busy sorting through music."

"I see."

"The staff at The Lion can vouch for me being there from six."

Yvonne made a note. "I may need to speak with you again, Mister McCready."

"Aye, well, you know where you can find me."

"Can I have your mobile number?"

He wiped his hands down the front of his jeans. "Sure. Why not? Do you have a pen?"

She handed him her pen and notepad.

"Thanks."

"Where do you go rock climbing?" she asked, watching as he scrawled his phone number.

"I've rock climbed all over Wales, Scotland, Ireland and France. I try to have at least one holiday abroad each year and include rock climbing."

"Where in Wales?"

"Rhobell Fawr is my favourite place. You get a lovely view of the Mawddach. Do you know it?"

She shook her head.

"Have you been to Snowdonia? If you haven't, go. You won't regret it." He handed her back her notepad.

Yvonne placed it in her handbag, along with her iPad. "Thank you for your time."

He shrugged. "You're welcome."

MARK TURNER WAS NOT without his supporters. They had been just as vocal as his critics on social media.

Yvonne needed their input for a more rounded knowledge of the victim, and to investigate what they knew about the cave.

Amongst the names they had collected was that of John Blackman.

A lifelong friend of Mark's, John was a thirty-three-year-old maths teacher at Newtown High School. He had commented on Facebook and YouTube to support the things his friend said about the finding of the cave, though he had not been there to witness the discovery himself.

He agreed to meet the DI on a break, in a room across the corridor from his classroom. The kettle was already on when reception staff showed Yvonne in.

"DI Giles?" He held out a hand. "Would you like a cup of tea?"

She accepted his offered shake, taking in his open gaze, handsome face, and dark, mussed up hair. "Yes, I'm Yvonne Giles. I would love a cup of tea. Thank you for agreeing to see me. I realise you must be busy." She accepted a chair, whose size and appearance suggested it had come from the classroom.

He poured water onto the teabags, stirring each mug. "Milk? Sugar?"

"Just milk, thank you," she answered, reaching for the plain white mug he handed over.

Once seated, she had a view of the yard. The hub of the school. It was dead now, but would quickly fill when the bell went.

He placed his mug on the table as he sat. "We have had exams, and are now in the middle of marking, and getting ready for the summer holidays. It will calm down, soon. You wanted to speak to me about Mark?" He sighed. "Dreadful business. He and I go back a long way. I cannot believe he has gone." His eyes dropped to the floor.

The DI gave him a moment to gather his thoughts. "I understand you were best friends?"

"Yes, we were." He lifted his eyes to hers. "We had been since primary school. We have always had each other's backs."

"I see. And you hiked together, am I right?"

"Many, many times over the years. We went on our first hike, aged ten. It was only to the next housing estate, but everybody has to start somewhere." He laughed. "Boy, back then, we thought we were sophisticated, filling our school backpacks with sandwiches and cans of pop." His eyes became wistful. "In some ways, it seems like only yesterday. Hard to believe it was twenty-three years ago."

"His death must have been a shock." Yvonne tilted her head, her gaze steady.

"I still expect him to send me a text, or start face-timing me."

"Did he do that often?"

"At least, once a day, yes."

"Did you hear from him that Saturday?"

He nodded. "I got a text from him in the morning, saying he was intending to look for the cave. That was the cave he discovered a few weeks before."

"What did you think about that?"

"Well, I wished him luck with it. I couldn't go myself. My wife is pregnant with our second child and getting close. I didn't want to be in the wilderness if she had a show. I popped out for some bits and pieces. I was in town when he texted."

"I see. I understand you supported him in arguments about the cave on social media?"

"I did. Of course I did. I mean, if Mark told me something was the case, I had no reason to doubt it. Why would I? And why would he make something like that up? There are too many people out there willing to troll others and put them down. It's almost like a sport to some folks. The armchair trolls. Of course I supported him and I would do it again. Well, if he was still here... obviously."

"What did you think when you heard someone had murdered him? What were your first thoughts?"

"Well, disbelief, obviously. I mean... Why? Why would someone do something like that to Mark? He was one of the nicest men around. He didn't have a nasty bone in his body.

Sure, he was exuberant, competitive, even, but harmless and with a heart of gold."

"Did you have any idea who might be responsible? Are you aware of anyone bearing a grudge? Did he have enemies?"

"None that I am aware of. I mean, he had occasional disagreements, sure. Who doesn't? But that wouldn't normally lead to someone's death. I think it most likely a stranger murdered him. He was probably in the wrong place at the wrong time." He shrugged. "I don't see any other explanation."

"What about the discussions you just mentioned, the ones on social media? Was anyone who commented on those of particular concern?"

He shook his head. "Er, well, I hadn't even considered that as an option. You think those comments have resulted in his death?"

"I don't know, Mister Blackman, I was just wondering if you thought anyone's comments vehement enough to be noteworthy."

He rubbed his chin. "Well, to be honest, I hadn't really thought about it. I mean, there was a lot of banter back and forth between the two camps, those who supported and those who didn't, but heated discussions are commonplace on social media. Do you think that someone he argued with on the net actually came here and killed him?"

"It's one possibility. I am not saying that happened. We are looking at all options but, yes, that is something we have been considering."

"I see." His expression became grave. "Wow. I mean, I got caught up in those discussions too, on Mark's side." He looked at her, wide-eyed. "I have a son and my wife is pregnant."

She held up a hand. "I am not saying that you are at risk. Take your usual sensible precautions. Lock your windows and doors at night, but there is nothing to suggestion you are any more likely to get hurt than anyone else. The murderer killed Mark on a hike, in what looked like a targeted attack. We don't yet have a motive for his killing. We shouldn't jump to conclusions. However, if you see anything suspicious or have a reason to fear for yourself or your family, then please contact us. She handed him her card. I barely ever switch off my mobile."

Blackman leaned back in his chair, rubbing his face. "Someone threatened him a few months back. I am trying to remember exactly when. It happened after Christmas, but I am struggling to recall how close it was to Easter. I think it was before, but I can't be sure."

Yvonne took out her pen and pad. "Mark was threatened?"

He nodded. "Yes, he was."

"Who threatened him? What did they say, exactly?"

"Well, I wasn't there, so didn't witness it myself. It was something Mark told me over a beer, after a hike, one afternoon around Easter time."

"What did Mark say had happened?"

"It was something to do with his ex-girlfriend, Sally. Her current boyfriend made the threats."

"What are their names, do you know?"

"Er, the ex is Sally Jenkins, and her boyfriend, the guy who made the threats, is Roy Joseph."

"What did Roy Joseph say to Mark?"

"He accused Mark of emotional abuse towards Sally, when she was Mark's girlfriend. I don't know the specifics, you would have to ask Roy, himself, but he threatened to do Mark in. It was on a night out in Newtown."

"So, another incident, on an evening after drinking. Would I be right in thinking this was a pattern of behaviour? Getting into altercations on nights out?"

Blackman shook his head. "Look, I can understand why you might think that way. It sounds like that, but it wasn't, really. We have been on many, many nights out and not gotten into arguments or fights. It's just that there have been one or two recent ones. I thought you should have all the information."

She nodded. "Thank you, and this is the sort of thing I need to know about. How do I find Sally and Roy?"

"Sally, works as a gym instructor at Maldwyn Sports centre, and Roy is unemployed, I think. He lost his job at the abattoir in Llanidloes. I believe he wasn't coping very well with the early starts. They had to let a few people go anyway because the work is seasonal, and he had clocked up more late starts and absences than most. They didn't renew his contract."

"When was this?"

"I think he lost his job in February or March."

"So just before he threatened Mark?"

"That is correct, yes."

"Is there anyone who can corroborate what you are saying? Anyone else who might have overheard the threats made?"

Blackman shrugged. "I honestly don't know. Like I say, Mark was out with friends having drinks in bars that night. The threat happened in one of those bars. I don't remember which, and I wasn't there, so cannot tell you if anyone else overheard."

"I see." Yvonne mused to herself about the murder weapon being one normally used in food prep. Perhaps it had come from the abattoir. She made a note to check with forensics and the abattoir for potential origins of the garrotte.

Blackman checked his watch. "Only five minutes to the end of my free period, I'm afraid."

She stood. "That is not a problem. Thank you for your time. Please call me if you think of anything else."

He nodded, offering his hand again. "I will."

SALLY JENKINS WAS serious about exercise. Everything, from her yellow vest top and black lycra shorts, to her toned muscles and shiny skin, suggested she worked out at least once, and likely several times a day.

Though not overweight, the DI felt flabby in comparison. She made a mental note to go swimming soon and, perhaps, ask Tasha to accompany her.

As Yvonne surveyed Sally's face, it was clear she had not shed many tears. If she had loved Mark, she was well over it now.

Sally lifted her sports bag and came over, as Yvonne placed coins into the coke machine in the atrium of Maldwyn sports centre. "Are you the police officer?" She tossed the words forth like she had better things to do. The accompanying sigh and wandering gaze underlined this.

Yvonne took a couple of seconds to reply, waiting for those travelling eyes to pay attention. "I am DI Yvonne Giles, yes. And you must be Sally Jenkins?"

"I am. Is this about Mark?" Sally glared at the DI, as though annoyed that the detective had interrupted her day at all.

Yvonne wondered if this was a defence mechanism. "It is about his death, yes."

Sally's face softened, taking the DI by surprise. "Silly sod, he was always putting himself out there. It's funny, when we were together, I was always afraid he would fall off something, or get stuck somewhere. I wasn't expecting, or even thinking, of his being murdered. That possibility never entered my head."

"Of course."

"He must have been very strong, whoever did this. Mark was no pushover."

"How long were you a couple for?"

"Three years, give or take. We lived together for most of that. I moved in with him after knowing him only six weeks."

"Wow, that was quick."

"Yes, I suppose it was. Maybe that was the problem."

"Was it a stormy relationship?"

Sally drew her head back. "What makes you ask that?"

"I understand your current boyfriend accused Mark of emotional abuse against you."

Sally's cheeks coloured.

"Was it true?"

The girl looked at the floor.

"Sally?"

"It was, and it wasn't."

"Meaning what?"

"Well, he liked to have control of the money. He liked to know what was coming in and going out. We had a joint bank account, but he didn't like me spending money without running it past him."

"Oh dear, I am sorry to hear that. Did you guys have debts?"

She sighed. "We had a couple of thousand pounds of debt, on top of the mortgage for the flat."

"Might that be why he was trying to keep a handle on things? Where did the debt come from?"

"Catalogue debts, credits cards, that sort of thing."

"Were you responsible for the deficit?"

Sally pursed her lips, her eyes narrowing as though she was unsure if she should answer that question.

"Was the debt yours?" Yvonne's gaze was steady.

Sally bit her lip. "Yes." She nodded. "I had run up most of it before Mark and I got together. My salary from this place is reasonable, I was just tempted a lot by offers online. You start off with little bits of debt and those little bits become a mountain."

Yvonne nodded. "Do you still owe money? You know you can get help from Citizen's advice. Get it deferred, even wiped."

"I know that. I am better at managing my money now, having gotten something from my relationship with Mark."

"Why did you guys split up?"

"Because of my work as a gym instructor, I get a lot of male attention. Mark found that hard to deal with. Cards and things being sent to our house, guys walking past the garden gate to see if I was home."

Yvonne tilted her head.

"I don't encourage it." Sally sighed. "I don't have to."

"Who walked out on whom?"

"I walked out on Mark. I hated the arguments. He never hurt me or anything. And he would always apologise after a row. I guess my heart just wasn't into the relationship after a while. There wasn't enough in it for me to stay. I think our decision to live together was hasty. We knew it after about six months. We just didn't discuss it, like we should have done."

The DI knew better than to say anything.

"It took me longer to agree to move in with Roy."

"That's Roy Joseph, your current partner?"

"Yes." Sally checked her watch. "He'll be on his way to the station. You wanted to speak to him today?"

Yvonne nodded. "That's right, I will head back there after speaking with you."

Sally swapped shoulders with her bag. "Is there anything more you need to know?"

"I wanted to ask you about an incident we've been told about."

"What incident?" Sally's eyes narrowed. "What do you mean?"

"Your boyfriend, Roy, threatened Mark sometime around Easter according to witnesses. Do you know anything about that? I believe you were present, and it occurred while you were all out drinking in a bar in Newtown."

"Oh, that." Sally puffed her cheeks out as she exhaled, exaggerating the sound.

"So, it happened?"

"Yes, it happened. It was silly. Something and nothing. Banter that got out of hand. You know how it is."

"No, I don't. I was hoping you might explain."

"Well, you can expect some tension between partners and ex-partners. It happens. I didn't want Roy to go into the Buck. I could see some of Mark's friends outside having a smoke, and I guessed that he would be inside. Roy had had a few, I guessed that Mark would also have had a few, and it worried me there could be trouble."

"But Roy went inside?"

"Yes, he did. At first, it was all fine. Both he and Mark stayed away from each other and were drinking with friends in their respective corners."

"So, what happened?"

"I saw Mark heading to the bar, just as Roy was finishing his pint. I tried to distract Roy, but he was insisting on buying a round of drinks. We were drinking with three of his friends, all of whom were on pints."

"So Mark was at the bar when Roy got there?"

"Yes, and I don't know what they said to start the argument. Roy wouldn't talk about it after it happened. Next thing I know, they are shouting at each other and Roy was threatening to do Mark in."

"I see." Yvonne made notes.

"He didn't mean it. He said the words in anger. The following morning, he really regretted it. Roy is not a violent man. He didn't really want to harm Mark. He just lost his temper. It was a spur-of-the-moment thing, and one that he regretted. Is that why you have asked him into the station?"

"Yes, it is." The DI checked her watch. "He will be with my sergeant, Dewi Hughes now. I ought to get back."

Sally pulled a face. "If you think that my Roy killed Mark, you are very much mistaken."

Yvonne gave one nod of her head. "I'll let you get on Ms Jenkins. I'll let you know if we need to speak with you again."

AS EXPECTED, Roy Joseph was at the station, accompanied by Dewi, who had furnished him with coffee and a sandwich.

Yvonne apologised for arriving late and asked Dewi to show Joseph to an interview room, while she grabbed a much-needed toilet visit.

When she rejoined them, they were both seated and

Dewi introduced the informal interview, having explained to the interviewee that they would record the session.

Roy Joseph sported thick, black brows that gave his face an air of strength and focus. As he asked the detectives what the interview was about, the brows formed an almost perfect V.

"Thank you for agreeing to see us, Mister Joseph." Yvonne took her seat, sorting her paperwork such that she could see what she needed to.

"Mister Joseph sounds a bit too formal. You can call me Roy, you know."

The DI nodded. "Thank you, Roy. I shall."

He grunted.

Yvonne wasn't sure if it was a response or whether he was clearing his throat. "I asked you here, because we are investigating the death of a local man, Mark Turner."

"Yes, I guessed it would be something to do with that when you said it was about an incident at Easter."

"So, you remember the incident, then?"

"Of course I do."

"Can you tell us, in your own words, what happened?"

"Well, I was out in town with my partner, Sally, and a few friends. We were going around the pubs, having a few drinks."

"Yes."

"I think we had been to two or three other pubs already, when we arrived at The Buck Hotel for more drinks."

"Go on."

"Mark Turner was in there. He was my partner's ex-boyfriend."

"And, what happened?"

"Well, nothing, initially. We were each drinking with our

friends, and the atmosphere in the pub was pretty good. It was lively, but all good banter."

"I see…"

"Well, it was time for me to go to the bar and, well, he was there. I don't know how, but he gets… got my back up almost every time I saw the guy. He accused me of leaving rude comments on his social media posts."

"And had you?"

"No. Well, not exactly. He had split with Sally six months before, but was still following her posts and liking stuff and trying to interact with her. His attention was unwanted by Sally, and I had commented to this effect in reply to his postings, and warned him that Sally would block him if he continued."

"Was Sally not capable of telling him herself?" Yvonne raised an eyebrow.

"She was, but he hadn't listened when Sally asked him to back off. I just thought the message might have been stronger, coming from me."

"Could she not just have blocked him?"

"I suggested that to her, but she didn't want to. She said that would take it too far, because they had been partners, so should be civil. To be honest, though, I thought blocking him to be the best option. Sally just didn't agree."

"Were you worried in case they got back together?"

"What? No, of course I wasn't. Why would I be?" The V was back in the brows.

"Because sometimes ex-partners get back together."

"I didn't feel threatened, if that is what you mean. Sally loves me. She loved me, so I didn't feel insecure."

"Hmm. What happened after he asked you about your comments on social media?"

"I told him I thought he was trying to manipulate Sally

like he had during their relationship. I told him it was emotional abuse and I wouldn't be happy if he continued."

"And what did he say to that?"

"He asked me what I intended to do about it. I told him if he carried on, he would find out."

"Is that all you said?"

"Pretty much, yes."

"You didn't threaten to do him in?"

"What? No, of course I didn't."

"You are sure about that?"

"I'm sure."

"Where were you the Saturday before last?"

"Oh, come on,... Seriously?" His brows V'd, again.

"Well, where were you?"

"I was out looking for work."

"Ah, yes. I was told you lost your job at the abattoir. I was sorry to hear that."

"Really? Why would you care whether I lost my job?"

"I'm a detective. I'm not heartless, Roy."

"Yeah well, yes, I lost my job. They let me go because the starts were early in the morning and I am not good in the mornings. Never have been. I shouldn't have worked there to begin with. Still, you live and learn, right?"

"I guess so. Are you still looking for work?"

"I am. We're surviving on Sally's money at the moment. And, when you get used to two salaries coming in, it's tough."

"I bet. So, getting back to the incident in the Buck. What happened after you threatened Mark?"

"We left. To be honest, I was already turning for the exit when I made the remark. I decided I didn't want another round of drinks in there. The atmosphere would have been awful, and I could see that Sally was becoming upset. I thought it best to leave. Mark shouted something after us, but I didn't hear what it was. I was already heading out the door."

"I see. Did you see Mark again after that?"

He shook his head. "No, I don't think so."

"Tell me, Roy, do they use cheese wires at the abattoir?"

"Sometimes, yes. There's a food packaging division. Why do you ask?"

Yvonne pushed her seat back. "Thank you for coming in, Roy. That concludes my questions, for now."

"Am I free to go?"

"Yes, you have always been free to go."

"I hope you find his killer," he said, running his hand through his hair. "I mean that."

5

HOLES

Ben Phillips checked his harness and ropes for tears, wear and defects, tugging at the clips to check for weaknesses. It wouldn't do to find problems on site. Satisfied, he clipped the roll of rope to his belt, checked the LED lamp on his helmet, and that he had a spare battery pack.

At forty-five, he knew he was nearing the end of his caving career as his fitness levels dropped. But, while he still enjoyed and felt good about it, he would continue exploring the underworld while gifting his extensive knowledge to others. It also gave him a welcome break from the hospitality business, and the hotel he ran jointly with his wife.

There wasn't much of the natural geology he hadn't delved into over the twenty-six years of his favourite hobby. He was easily the most experienced of his group, and the one they all turned to when concerned or when needing advice. He gave the others the confidence they needed to push themselves, something they had always taken pride in. They led the way for many other cavers to follow.

He put a thumb up to Brian, showing all was well.

Brian Taylor, at forty, was the next most experienced of the group. With twenty-two years under his belt, he too had explored much of the local terrain and would be the one to take over the lead were anything to happen to Ben. He brought up the rear, checking those ahead of him were coping okay and helping anyone who got stuck. There was always some risk when potholing and caving. The idea was to minimise it and to prepare for any untoward consequences. Failing that, the Cave Rescue Teams were among those that might come out to save the day, something Brian prayed would not be necessary.

He waved back to Ben and threw the sky hook into a small backpack. He, too, checked his helmet lamp and tackle before strapping on knee and elbow pads over a neoprene suit.

Brian knew the holes they explored today would be wet. The neoprene would exclude the water and dry out quickly, keeping them warm as the temperatures would be significantly colder underground. Hypothermia was a constant threat and, as a paramedic, he would be responsible for the health of the group, should anything go wrong. He was the one keeping an eye out for slurred speech or acetone-smelling breath, signs that someone was suffering severe effects of the cold. He would deal with any sprains or other injuries and ensured the first aid kit was always current and fully stocked.

He and Ben made for a well-led team.

The other two members comprised twenty-eight-year-old council worker, Diane Metcalfe, and thirty-four-year-old Tim Wilson, a bus-driver originally from Liverpool, now living in Brecon.

All four team members knew each other's strengths and

weaknesses, having been caving as a fixed team for eight years. Firm friends, they trusted one another implicitly.

On this trip, they were heading for the Brasgyll gorge, off the River Elwy, which contained many holes and fissures in the rock, some of which remained unexplored.

They had sought relevant permissions, as the caves were on an estate in private ownership.

The downside of this location was the difficulty in obtaining accurate GPS in some cave systems. The area was beautiful, however, and would provide ample excitement for their caving trip.

As Tim fired up the truck for their brief drive to the gorge, Ben's mind drifted to when he was a boy of twelve. The tales he heard of caves off the River Elwy were what had first interested him in spelunking, the affectionate term for what they did.

Ben listened, wide-eyed, as his uncle told tales of the Victorian explorers who had left their mark on the larger caves, cataloguing several of them. He couldn't wait to explore himself. He had been back many times since then but, today, they would go into one he had not yet explored. A newly discovered fissure with a crawl tunnel going into the mountain. They would need to be on their game and leave plenty of removable markers to find their way back. It was not unusual for cavers to find themselves lost in a network of tunnels. They would take no chances.

Their first port of call would be to the estate office at Cefn, to sign a disclaimer. Then on for their adventure. Ben had brought his pocket HD video recorder to document parts of their journey.

~

THE VIEW STRETCHED OUT LANGUOROUSLY BELOW, on and on for miles.

This vantage point was like another world. Somewhere below, life carried on as usual but, up where they were, time slowed perceptibly. It relegated cares to another place and time.

Yvonne raised her hands above her head, stretching on tiptoes to plunge her fingers into the sky.

"Spectacular, isn't it?" Tasha caught her up from the footpath. "What do you think?"

A four-mile hike had taken them above Aberdovey, looking out over the tiny boats on the Dyfi estuary, and on over towards Borth and Aberystwyth. It had taken them just over two hours to get there, but the time and effort had been worth it. They had taken Cooper Street out of Aberdovey, under the railway bridge, and it hadn't been long before the breath-taking sea views opened up. But here, at the top, with the panoramic view over the town, this was special.

Yvonne filled her lungs with the salty sea air. "It's amazing, Tasha!"

"Isn't it just?" Tasha paused for breath. "I knew you would like it, DI Giles."

The DI grinned. "I love it when you call me that."

Tasha put her arm around her waist. "I knew you would."

"My worries have melted away." Yvonne smiled. "How do you do that?"

Tasha placed a soft peck on her cheek. "Magic."

The DI laughed, pulling away to take in more of the view.

Tasha followed, standing behind her, and once more placing her arms around her waist, chin on Yvonne's shoulder. Inside her pocket, a tiny box burned a hole. The psychologist longed to give the contents to her partner. Perhaps now was the right moment.

She moved to Yvonne's side, her countenance more serious, muscles tense. She pulled the compact package from her jacket pocket. "Yvonne, I-"

"We're investigating a horrible murder." The DI announced, her eyes fixed on the estuary, her thoughts elsewhere.

"Er, are you, really?" Tasha paused, her fist closing over the box.

"Yes. A man found garrotted in a field."

"Oh." Tasha pushed the receptacle back in her pocket, her breathing uneven. She cleared her throat. "When was this?"

"The Saturday before last." Yvonne sighed. "We think he was on a hike looking for a cave when he was murdered."

"I see. Not good." Tasha chewed the inside of her cheek, the sinking feeling in her gut gradually replaced by a professional curiosity. "Do you have any idea who did it?"

The DI shook her head. "Not yet. He'd had several arguments during the six months leading up to his death, but none of these stand out as particularly significant. A few heated debates on social media."

"What were the debates about?"

"The cave he was looking for." Yvonne pushed stray hair back from her face. "He told everyone he found a cave in an area not particularly known for them. There were people who doubted, and even took exception to, what he was saying. The social media arguments resulted from that. He made many of the followers incredulous by asserting that the cave had made his body shake. I think that was the kicker. The thing that turned even some of his supporters against the story."

The DI continued. "We think he was on his way back to the area in which he'd found the cave when someone killed him. He was retracing his footsteps, looking to gather evidence. He may have had his video camera with him, as we didn't find it at his flat, but it wasn't with the body either. We believe the killer or killers took it."

"I see."

Overhead, gulls swooped and cawed.

"It's been weighing on your mind." Tasha placed a hand on the DI's shoulder. "I nearly asked you at breakfast if something was troubling you."

"I'm sorry, Tasha." Yvonne sighed. "Here we are at this super location, I am with my most favourite person in the world, and I am thinking about work. It will never do." She smiled, taking the psychologist's hand. "Come on. Let's move on round. Take in more of this view."

6

SPELUNKING

Twenty-eight-year-old Diane Metcalfe got lost in her own thoughts during the truck ride to Brasgyll Gorge. She allowed the wooded hills and water-forged valleys to wash over her eyes and brain, soothing both like ice-cold juice soothes the insides on a blistering day. Different scenery. Different mind-set.

She needed this trip. Needed it more than she would ever admit, having spent the last two months feeling lower than she had in her life.

A second failed round of IVF treatment had left her and her thirty-year-old husband Paul devastated, their marriage under strain.

All those months of hormone injections; temperature checks; embryo insertions, and hiding it all from friends, whilst organising flexitime absences with bosses, and dealing with the subsequent accusatory looks from colleagues. All for nothing.

Perhaps the worst thing was having to smile while having lunch in the canteen, in Llandrindod Wells County Council offices, like everything was fine. Having a mundane conversation with colleagues, nodding now and then, whilst staring out of the plate-glass windows towards the fountain at the front of the building. Imagining she was anywhere but in that place. Imagining herself in a cave somewhere with the three best friends accompanying her on this journey. In this truck.

Paul had been her haven, initially. They had leaned on each other. Until the cracks developed. The inevitable fissures opening up as the pressure and self-recriminations mounted. She blamed herself for what she saw as her useless body. He blamed himself for the long hours bringing projects together only to sell them on, being not yet big enough or wealthy enough to start his own property portfolio. And, meanwhile, he and his wife hoped to start a family in their semi-detached, two-bedroom house in Newtown.

Their daily commutes didn't help. Both in opposite directions, Diane working in Llandrindod Wells, twenty-seven miles to the south of Newtown, while Paul worked in the North, and across the Shropshire border in the Shrewsbury and Telford areas. His daily commute, anything up to two hours each way.

Yes, they had been through enough, for now. They talked of a third and final attempt. Their doctor said he would look into whether further funding was available, but had warned that, this time, they might have to finance it themselves. Another blow to already fragile energies.

And all the while, she and the rest of her Human Resources team were responsible for nearly six thousand other council staff, all of whom had their own work-life balance to manage. Their own difficulties and crosses to bear.

Caving was her escape. Her go-to when all else crumbled around her. Had been since she was fifteen and explored her first cave on a school trip, and seen stalactites and stalagmites for herself, while gazing in awe at the coloured striations in the rocks. She loved the thrill and excitement of delving into the unknown. The unseen.

TIM WILSON HAD BEEN a caver most of his life. His grandfather having started off his passion, when Tim was only seven years old.

Now, at thirty-four, he had a solid seventeen years' experience in the business, and knew how to pull his weight, should anything untoward happen. There was always a risk with caving, but he had faith in the team, and in Brian's ability to lead it. This instilled in him the confidence to reach out and explore spaces he might not have otherwise.

It kept him in shape, his day-job as a bus driver being rather more sedentary. He had witnessed the bellies of some of his colleagues growing almost daily, not helped by long shifts and snatched meals of fast food. He didn't want the same happening to him. Caving was hard, physical work. It kept the weight off.

BRIAN PLACED the first aid kit back in his pack. He had checked it twice, but felt compelled to go through it one more time. He had a sense that something was different about this day, and they would call upon his skills. A premonition he hoped was wrong.

Accidents had been a rare thing for this group. Long may that continue, he thought.

Perhaps what had spooked him was a comment made to

him when working as part of his paramedic team, two nights before. A middle-aged man had fallen from a ladder, broken his arm and gone into cardiac arrest.

He and his partner opened up his shirt, shaved his chest, and applied a defibrillator, pads either side. They success-fully shocked the guy back.

They saved the patient's life that night, but it showed how easily a relatively minor accident could escalate into a life-threatening situation.

His caving team carried a defibrillator in the back of their truck. It was too big a pack for them to carry into the tunnels. Brian mused, not for the first time, that it wasn't much use to them if they had no access to it where they were most likely to need it. Chances were they wouldn't have time to retrieve it and he would rely on his CPR skills, alone. Luckily, the members of his group were fit, but you just never knew what might happen.

They arrived in the gorge as the sun came out from behind a thick cloud.

The resulting vista took his breath, the sunlight bouncing off the surface of the stream flowing in the mini canyon, highlighting the colours in the rock.

This was a day to be spelunking.

7

KILLER'S LAIR

The yawn made his jaw click as though about to dislocate. He checked his watch. He had been at this trawling lark for nearly four hours. He ought to have something to eat. He couldn't operate on fresh air. Spotting potential victims was hungry work. He had identified his next quarry and, conveniently for him, they had set out an itinerary for their upcoming trips. How helpful.

He leaned back in his chair, a self-satisfied smirk curling his lips. It didn't harm to do a little baiting. Having verbal sport with them beforehand. Work them up, make them rude against their will and natural inclination and, meanwhile, he could become piqued enough to kill.

A familiar ping showed that one of them had replied. They couldn't resist. Questioning their extensive knowledge would always irritate them. He was good at that. Knew how to goad someone. He always found a way in, especially doing it in public.

'What do you mean, you doubt anyone has completed that network?'

He had riled this one. 'The passages are too narrow. You couldn't have gotten through.'

'But I am telling you that we did. We crossed right through that mountain. We did it. Why can't you accept that?'

I think you want the credit for something you didn't achieve because it sounds good. Maybe you want to impress your girlfriend? Think she'll be all over you for this, huh?'

'Who are you? Why are you doing this?'

I'm a spelunker. I know caves. I know what is possible and what isn't. I know when someone is lying.'

'I will report this to the moderator. You are a troll.'

'What a shame, the moderator appears to be asleep.'

'I'll leave you talking to yourself.'

'That's because you lost the argument. You know that system is too narrow. It's not on to mislead people the way you are. There are youngsters here who are listening to your every word.'

'You have nothing better to do. I'm going.'

'You know I'm right. You have no arguments.'

'We did it.'

'You got video footage?'

'Are you crazy? We couldn't film in that bit. We were squeezing through. How would we record it?'

'Then it didn't happen.'

'Un-bloody-believable.'

'My thoughts exactly.'

He got up from his chair, arching backwards to stretch his vertebrae, hearing them crack as they realigned. That was enough baiting, for now. Timing was everything. For all their threats, if he left now, they likely wouldn't get him booted. That gave him the chance to play again tomorrow. And play he would. There was a long way to go.

He went through his gear. Waterproofs, lamps, rope, helmet, rucksack. He had food, water, maps, compass and GPS. He left nothing to chance. Never would.

If he was to set a trap, he had to know the caves and tunnels better than those he sought to ensnare. He would leave them wishing they could rip out the tongues that had uttered harsh words or, even, cut off the fingers that typed them.

8

CLUES

Yvonne opened the interim forensic report, analysing both the murder scene, and the garrotte used as the weapon.

It confirmed the wire as one used for food preparation and had originated with a company in France called Fante's. What they did not know was where the killer purchased it, but that was in hand, and suspected to be a major online retailer. Spectroscopy showing the exact molecular makeup would help determine a batch number from which they would attempt to follow the chain from manufacture, through supply, and on to the purchaser.

The spectroscopic traces were likely being generated even as she read and compared with samples provided voluntarily by the company. It was a long shot, but one that could furnish concrete evidence to support the conviction of the murderer.

IN THE MEANTIME, Dewi ran checks on the social media discussions, that took place in both YouTube and Facebook, on Mark Turner's posts about the cave.

One profile, in particular, stood out. Pierre Gram.

Pierre had been vocal on both social media sites. His comments appeared to goad Turner to return to the cave and provide evidence not only of its existence but also of the tremors it had generated in his body.

A preliminary skim of Gram's profile showed it was less than a year old and had limited numbers of friends and followers.

"So, no family information for this Pierre Gram, Dewi?" Yvonne sighed, pursing her lips.

"I'm afraid not, ma'am. It looks very much to me as though he set up this account for trolling, using false information. He hides the details like his IP address behind firewalls that are constantly changing."

"Like the dark web?"

"Very much like that, ma'am, yes." Dewi read further down his notes. "He relishes starting arguments. He knows which buttons to press, even with those resistant to engaging with him."

"Is he commenting on other people's posts?"

Dewi nodded. "On cavers' and potholers' posts, yes. He seems to be fairly knowledgeable, suggesting he has personal experience of spelaeology."

"Spelaeology?"

"Spelunking. Potholing, ma'am."

"Got you." Yvonne nodded. "Would make sense. If he has something to do with the murder, then I suspect he knows where to find that cave. Are all the posts on which he has commented in Wales?"

"They are, yes."

"Okay, well, let's keep a watch on him. I want to know who he is communicating with and why. He may have nothing to do with our case, but he has a French-sounding name, and we know the murder weapon was French. That doesn't imply a connection but add it too the goading behaviour, and it adds up. It may be a tentative lead, but it's a lead. Well done, Dewi, keep on it."

Her sergeant placed the papers under his arm, and his pen behind his ear. "Will do."

DAI HANDED YVONNE SEVERAL PHOTOGRAPHS. "They found a folder with newspaper cuttings in Mark's flat."

"Go on."

"Well, the articles were all connected to various scams on the elderly. Someone defrauded one couple of one-hundred-and-twenty thousand pounds."

"No way..."

"Yes. The perp told them he would invest their money for high returns. He sent them monthly updates with generous interest payments and they believed their money to be growing well."

"But it wasn't?"

"Exactly, the perp had the money paid into a community bank in Cardiff, supplying false identification, to open the account. He told the bank the money was from the sale of his dead parent's home, and he wanted the interest on that money to benefit the community. The bankers thought all their Christmases had come at once."

"Was the perp caught?"

"No, ma'am. By the time the couple smelled a rat, it was eleven months later. The offender had withdrawn all funds into an offshore account, two months before, using false company details. From there, he laundered it through several accounts and most of the money disappeared. Serious Fraud investigators are still chasing it down."

"So, why would Mark Turner have cuttings of this?"

"That's what we're wondering, ma'am."

"Get onto Tuner's bank. Find out if any unusual transactions occurred over the last eighteen months. If he was doing anything dodgy, I want to know about it."

Dai nodded. "I'll get on it straight away."

"Thanks, we want full print-outs of everything. Also, how many bank accounts did he have? Let Serious Fraud know, especially if you find anything they ought to be aware of."

"Will do, ma'am."

"Superb work, Dai."

"Thank you."

9

PLANS THWARTED

T hat evening, aromatic odour greeted Yvonne as she opened the front door.

She lifted her nose to sniff the air and, tossing her keys onto the table in the hall, wandered through to the kitchen. "Wow, that smells amazing. What is it? Mexican?"

"Chicken fajitas." The psychologist grinned. I flamed the bell peppers before slicing and adding them in.

"Amazing aroma." Yvonne took off her coat, throwing it over the back of a bar stool. "I'm going for a shower, will that be okay as regards your timing?"

Tasha took off her apron. "That will be perfect. They are in the oven. I will carry them, still sizzling, to the table in around ten minutes."

The DI grinned, taking in her partner's shining eyes, perfect makeup, and smart white shirt. "You look beautiful, Tasha. Is this a special occasion? It's not your birthday...Anniversary?"

Tasha laughed, placing her hands on her hips. "Don't be cheeky. Don't I always look this good? Go get that shower."

When she returned, the DI found Tasha pouring merlot into two generous glasses.

"You're just in time. Take a seat, I'll bring the dishes to the table."

The cast iron receptacles hissed as the psychologist brought them through.

The salivating Yvonne had not realised how hungry she was. Now, she could not wait.

Tasha brought through bowls of guacamole, salsa, and sour cream.

Flat breads and lighted candles were the last additions to the table.

"Wow, I really am being spoiled here, Tasha, you are a star, and the best partner in the world. This table looks amazing."

The psychologist smiled, aware of the velvet box in her trouser pocket. She wanted the perfect moment. "Wine?" she asked, keeping her expression as relaxed as she could as the tension caused a tightening in her stomach.

The DI appeared oblivious, nodding at the wine, and patiently waiting for the psychologist to sit before tucking in.

Tasha had prepared lemon meringue pie and had decided that desert would be an agreeable time to take out the box. She took a deep breath to calm her nerves. Not long now.

The wine enhanced the flavour of the dish. Yvonne smiled at her partner. "My compliments to the chef. The food is excellent and the wine, perfect. What did I do to deserve you? I think you were a golden gift from the universe."

Tasha moved round. Her eyes had a depth and a warmth that lit her face. "I am the one with the gift." She put her hand to her pocket, just as Yvonne's mobile rang in the kitchen.

"Oh, no…" The DI sighed as she left to retrieve it from the countertop. "Not work now, please."

"Can you ignore it?" The psychologist tilted her head.

Yvonne shook hers. "I really ought to take it, Tasha. No-one calls me at dinnertime without a reason."

Tasha nodded, leaving the box in her pocket. "I understand." She watched as the DI gave several instructions down the phone, her face tense.

"I've got to go, Tasha. I am sorry. I know how much effort you put into this."

The psychologist placed a hand on Yvonne's shoulder. "It's okay, I will make you a take away fajita wrap while you get your coat on."

"It's another murder," the DI said in apology."

"I guessed as much." Tasha took Yvonne's meat dish and wraps to the kitchen. "I'll have a foil-wrapped package for you by the time you leave."

THE YOUNG VICTIM lay on top of his collapsed tent, his outdoor gear scattered around the outside as though someone had been through it, stealing anything they took a shine to.

"He's been dead at least several hours." Hanson approached the DI from the corpse.

Yvonne cast her eyes over the victim's belongings. "What was he doing camping here? It's not an official campsite."

Hanson shrugged, pushing a hand into the small of his back as he straightened. "People don't always stick to official camp sites. They ask the farmer for permission and set up camp. Maybe he was on his way to an event around here?"

"Well, there are no festivals going on, but we are on the edge of the Dolfor Moors." She pursed her lips. "I wonder if he was looking for Mark Turner's cave?"

"Sorry?" Hanson frowned.

"The guy we found dead a couple of weeks ago. He'd been trying to locate a cave he had found."

"Oh yes, I remember." Hanson nodded. "They garrotted this man, like the last. He put up a fight, though I do not think it lasted long. It looks like they disturbed him in his sleep. Tired and groggy, he wouldn't have been able to mount much of a defence."

"You think they killed him last night?"

Hanson nodded. "I would say so, yes. We will give you a better approximation as soon as we can. An educated guess based on what we see here, would be that they surprised him while he was sleeping, called him out of the tent, and grabbed him from behind. The first attempt at killing him looks to have been unsuccessful. The wire had dug in, but the victim fought him off, perhaps by elbowing the perpetrator in the gut. He wasn't successful at getting away a second time."

Yvonne shuddered. "No." She gazed into the black night beyond the police floodlights. Nothing out there, save for the grassed hills and the sheep whose eyes reflected the light back at her as they investigated the unusual activity taking place within the cordon.

The DI brought hers back to the sprawled male atop the mangled tent, going over his last moments in her mind. She had forgotten the chicken fajita, foil-wrapped with love by Tasha. She could not have eaten, anyway. Not after witnessing the bulging eyes in that young, blood-stained face. "He must be strong, the killer."

Hanson rubbed his stubble. "I would agree with that. Mark Turner, your first victim, was no pushover. He was lean and muscular. This perp is powerful. The alternative is that you have yourselves more than one murderer."

"God, I hope not." Yvonne sighed. "I'm worried this is a serial killer."

Hanson pulled his mask back over his mouth. "You might be right."

IT WAS A FURTHER two days before they had an identity for the victim.

Gareth Sheldon, originally from Birmingham, had moved with his family to Wales, fourteen months before. Aged nineteen, and known as Gary to his friends, he was studying catering at Newtown College and was popular amongst his peer group.

Dewi confirmed Gary had an interest in caving and had been one of Mark Turner's vocal supporters on social media. "I think he was looking for the cave to prove to dissenters, Turner was correct. Perhaps he felt it important since Mark had lost his life looking for it."

Yvonne nodded. "I think you may be right, Dewi. I also suspect someone else was watching social media and knew Gary was going on the hunt for it. Get digging, would you? Get us the names of all those commenting on Gary's posts regarding the cave. I would be particularly interested to know if Pierre Gram had been in contact with him."

"Will do." Dewi handed her a mug. "Get that coffee down you. I've a feeling you will need it."

10

GRIEF

Friday morning saw Yvonne tapping her feet, waiting for someone to open the door at a detached, red-brick house on New Road in Newtown. It was the home of Gary Sheldon, the latest victim of a garrotting on the Dolfor Moors, at only nineteen years old.

It would devastate his parents. It would have been hard, anyway, but even more so since their son was only just starting in life. His loss would have destroyed not only his future, but theirs as well.

She was about to give up and walk away, when the door opened and a dark-haired man of around forty-five years old motioned her in.

His movements stiff and shoulders hunched, he led her through the hallway.

She cleared her throat. "I'm Yvonne Giles, I've come-"

"I know." He continued walking, his back to her.

She closed her mouth. He wasn't for talking. She understood.

Luckily for the DI, his wife was more communicative. Though her red and swollen eyes suggested she would be better catching some much-needed rest. "I'm Diane, Gary's mum." She held out a hand which shook perceptibly. "Thank you for taking the time to come and see us."

Yvonne's heart went out to her as she took the offered hand, struck by how cold it was. She suspected that Diane Sheldon had not eaten for some time. "Pleased to meet you, Mrs Sheldon. I am sorry for your unimaginable loss."

Diane sighed. It shook her slight frame. "That's my husband, Derek," she said about the man who had left them alone. "He won't talk about it. Gary's loss is killing him."

The DI nodded. "I can quite understand. To lose a child is devastating, whatever age they are, but one so young..."

Diane crossed the floor of her open-plan kitchen-diner. "Gary was the light of our lives. There was never a dull moment when he was around. The house is now so... silent." She ran a hand through her straw-blonde hair, which brushed her shoulders. "I kept hoping you had found someone else's boy. That it was a mistake. That it wasn't our Gary. Until Derek went to identify his body. I couldn't have done that. I didn't want to see him hurt."

"I know." Yvonne put a hand on her shoulder. "My heart goes out to you."

"You'll have questions, I guess?" Diane's wide eyes appeared lost, as though she knew there were things to do, but had no idea where to start.

The DI guessed that Derek was in no state to help his wife or himself. "Is there anything I can do?" she asked. "Shall I put the kettle on for you? You look like you could use a cuppa."

Diane's eyes focussed. "Oh yes, tea, I should have offered."

Yvonne held up a hand. "No, no, honestly, I wouldn't have expected that. I am offering because you look like you need one. Something to eat probably wouldn't go amiss, either."

Diane shook her head. "I can't face anything. Not yet."

"Of course." Yvonne crossed to the kettle. "Where are your teabags?"

Mrs Sheldon reached for a cupboard above the DI, taking down a tin. "They're in here"

"Will your husband have one?"

Diane tilted her head. "We'll make him one. He will probably drink it while lost in his own thoughts."

"Have they offered you counselling?" Yvonne asked, as she began adding the teabags to three mugs.

"They told us about it and left leaflets, I haven't read any of them yet."

"No, it's too much for you to take in right now. You might find it helpful as time moves on. I don't believe I could think about it all at the moment, either. Even the smallest task can feel overwhelming after such a loss."

"Yes, you understand." Mrs Sheldon peered into Yvonne's eyes as she realised the DI was someone who had been there. Someone who had known similar pain.

Yvonne poured boiling water into the mugs. "Do you have milk and sugar?"

"Just milk for me. Derek likes his black."

The tea made, Yvonne leaned against the kitchen counter, while Diane took her husband's drink through. Eyes glazed, she thought about the adolescent whose parents had been so devastated, feeling thankful they had not had to witness what she had up on the moor.

"Are you ready for those questions?" she asked when Mrs Sheldon returned.

Diane nodded. "As I'll ever be."

Yvonne took out her notebook. "I'll be as succinct as I can."

"It's okay, ask what you need to." Mrs Sheldon sipped her tea. "I want my son's killer found. That's what matters to me. Ask away."

"Thank you. Had Gary been camping before, or was this trip unusual for him?"

"No. He'd enjoyed camping since he was young. He was two-and-a-half when we first took him to a campsite. He loved it right from the start. Seasides were his favourite, but he liked woods as well. There was no stopping him once he was old enough to plan his own trips. He usually told us where he was going, though."

"I see. Did he say anything to you about this trip? Did he tell you where he was going and why?"

"He said he would camp on the moors. I asked him not to, because of what happened up there, you know."

"You mean of the murder of Mark Turner?"

"Yes, he said he would be fine because there was still a lot of police activity in the area, and that you couldn't get much safer than that."

The DI nodded. "The moors cover an extensive area, unfortunately. His camp was a considerable distance from our cordons. There were no officers posted where we found him."

"I realise that now." Mrs Sheldon shook her head. "I wish I had persuaded him not to go. If only I had stopped him."

Yvonne placed a hand on her arm. "You can't blame yourself. He was old enough to make his own decisions. You did your best."

Dianne sighed, both hands wrapped around her mug, the contents of which she had barely touched.

"Did Gary tell you why he was camping up there?"

"He said he would find a cave, proving its existence, in memory of the man who died."

"Mark Turner."

"Yes, that's right."

"Did he know Mark, personally?"

Diane shook her head. "No, he knew about the cave because of following Mark online." Her eyes widened. "Was my son killed because of that cave?"

"Honestly? I don't know. It's an obvious interest in common with Mark, but it is too early to say, Mrs Sheldon. I can tell you that we will do everything in our power to get to the bottom of what happened and why."

Diane nodded. "Thank you."

"Will your husband be all right?"

"I'll go to him, in a while. He needs his space right now. I understand that."

"Mrs Sheldon, we'll need access to your son's belongings, and we'll be going through his online communications. We will need your permission to do some of these things."

"Whatever you need."

"May I ask, did your son have concerns about anyone in his social circle? Around town, or in the general area? I understand he was at college?"

"Yes, he was halfway through a catering course. Gary loved it at college and didn't mention problems, aside from the odd concern about making a particular grade. He had a pleasant set of friends. Some of them have been here to offer their condolences." Diane pointed to the cards on the counter.

"Of course. What about around town? Friends not associated with college? Anyone else?"

Mrs Sheldon thought for a moment. "He had other friends, but none that concerned him. They didn't scare him, if that's what you mean. And he wasn't into drugs or anything of that nature. He'd have a drink, that's about it."

"What about caving? Presumably, he had contacts within that world?"

"I think you'll find all of those on his Facebook page. I didn't see any of them. He would meet up with people from other areas in Wales. He'd head off on his motorbike, you know."

"Yes, we found his bike close to his tent. Did he have a video camera with him, do you know?"

"He did. He took his camera everywhere. I know he wouldn't have gone to find the cave without taking it to document and record the evidence."

"No, I suspected as much, Mrs Sheldon. Thank you for confirming that for me."

"You're welcome."

"I may have further questions as this investigation unfolds. Is it okay for me to contact you as and when I need to?"

"Yes, yes, of course. Please do, Inspector. Find my son's killer. Gary cannot rest in peace until you have."

"I will do everything I can, Mrs Sheldon, I promise."

"Thank you."

As Yvonne left the Sheldon's home, she pondered on their grief, hoping that Derek would open up and let his wife in, instead of shutting her out. They needed each other if they were to get through this.

11

PRECIOUS METAL

D r Shearer met Yvonne and Dewi at the entrance to Coleg Powys, the major college in Newtown, off the roundabout near the Mochdre Industrial Estate.

Sporting a brown tweed jacket and tie, he took them along several corridors before ushering them into an empty classroom.

Yvonne noted his open, warm expression and the flecks of dandruff in his greying hair, some of which lay like ash on his shoulders.

"Geoff Shearer," he said, holding out a hand to shake first Dewi's, then the DI's.

They introduced themselves.

"Thank you for seeing us," Yvonne began, eyes wandering to the glass windows on her right and over the full length of the well-lit space.

"We deliver the Welsh Baccalaureate here," he stated. "We offer geology up to 'A' level grade. If they wish to take it further, they go on to university."

The DI nodded. "It looks like a great environment to learn in. It's so luminous."

"It is. You said you wanted to talk about the local geology?" He pulled chairs out for the detectives.

"That's right." Yvonne seated herself, placing her bag on the floor next to her chair. "Particularly of the Dolfor Moors."

"We'd like your opinion on where, if anywhere on the moors, we might find a cave or caves," Dewi chimed in.

"Caves?" Shearer scratched his chin through his beard. "The area is not known for caves..."

"We know that, Doctor Shearer." Yvonne held his gaze. "But, were one to exist, what is the most likely location, would you say? Your professional opinion is all we need."

He grimaced.

The DI explained further. "We are trying to locate the cave a murder victim discovered on the moors. We think he was killed while looking for it a second time, two weeks after he first found it."

"Oh yes, I heard about the murder." Shearer sighed. "Such a waste of young life. Didn't another youngster also lose their lives up there recently?"

"Yes, they did." Yvonne took a map from her bag, pre-marked with the boundaries of their area of interest. "This is the general area. Can you help us?"

Shearer took the map from her, perusing it with his lips pursed. "Let's see, now... There are sandstone deposits in some of that land. It's on Ordovician and Silurian sedimentary rock. Those are the main formations in the area. There are around five metres of rock underneath deep peat soils and sandstone. Now there could, in theory, be caves somewhere in that sandstone but, equally, he may have stumbled on an old mine."

"A mine?" Yvonne leaned forward in her chair.

"Yes, they mined the rocks and sandstone in the nineteenth and early twentieth centuries for aggregates and building materials. The Romans were also active in the area, after zinc and lead, in the main. There has been a fair amount of mining in the area, actually. I read in the paper that your man was a hiker. If he wasn't a natural caver, then he may have mistaken an old mine entrance for a cave. That is possible, isn't it?"

The DI had to admit; she hadn't even considered that as a possibility. "Wouldn't an old mine have had its entrance filled in?" she asked.

"Not necessarily and, even if it did, flooding could have opened it up, or even a farmer making alterations to the land. Then there are cavers, and treasure hunters, who uncover things all the time."

"I see." Yvonne nodded. "Would you be able to suggest the likely location of old mines?"

"May I?" He pointed to the map, taking out a pen.

"By all means." The DI handed him the map.

Shearer marked out two areas in red ink. "I'd be looking in those places," he suggested. "However, if you give me a week, I can give you GPS co-ordinates for areas which might be more useful. I will consult with others, with a greater knowledge than myself, and get back to you."

Yvonne handed him her card. "That would be incredible, thank you."

Shearer rose from his chair. "I'll show you out."

TASHA PUT down the phone after having a conversation with seniors at the Met, who needed her help on a serial murder case.

She looked at her watch. Yvonne wouldn't be back for another two hours, and the psychologist would have to tell her she was going away again, something she didn't want to do. In fact, the timing could not be worse.

She thought about the box. Perhaps, she could leave it somewhere, in a drawer or some other place her partner would discover it. Leave it with a note.

Tasha dismissed this idea almost as soon as it entered her head. That was not the way to ask something so important and life-changing.

No, it would have to wait until the psychologist returned from London, if she didn't give it to her partner tonight. This was something she did not want to rush.

The DI had telephoned to explain she would work late, following a second murder. Yvonne would be tired and in need of a hot soak and food. It felt inappropriate to raise the subject at such a time.

The psychologist stared through the lounge window at the valley below, stretched out as far as the Shropshire Hills, her heart aching. Fate was mischievous.

12

POSTMORTEM

"So, what are we looking at?" Yvonne asked Hanson as she stared at the body of Gareth Sheldon, the deep wound from the Garrotte all too apparent.

"It's a carbon copy of the first murder, Yvonne. The same killer, or someone familiar with the first killer's methods, and who had a similar size and strength. I would lay odds on it being one person responsible for both killings."

The DI nodded. "I feared as much. What about time of death?"

"Early hours of the morning. I believe we are looking at a time between three and four am. I think the killer chose this, knowing his victim would be dazed from sleep and less capable of defending himself."

The DI could imagine the fear in Gary Sheldon's eyes. The dread. "I hope it was fast."

"It wouldn't have taken long. Not with the garrotte used."

"Another cheese wire?"

"Yes, another wire from Fante's."

Yvonne thought again of the social media character Pierre Gram. French name. Was that merely coincidence?

Or was this mysterious internet character the man they were looking for? "What about Gary's fingernails? Anything from those?"

"We found skin under them. Don't get too excited. We know the victim made one successful attempt to get the garrotte off. At least some, if not all, of that skin will be his. But, who knows, we may get another profile. I will keep you informed."

"Thank you." Yvonne sighed. "Gary's father may never recover from his loss, and his mother is putting a brave face on it, but her grief is palpable. Such a tragedy..."

"Find this killer, Yvonne. If anyone can, it's you. Stop this happening again."

I'll try, Roger. I'll try."

"COME IN!" Llewelyn called from the other side of the door.

Yvonne pushed it open, straightening her skirt. "You're working late, sir."

It was eight-thirty pm.

"I am, Yvonne." He pushed his glasses atop his head. "I can do that occasionally, you know."

"I'm sorry, sir. I didn't mean to imply-"

He held up his hand. "That's fine. Have you got five minutes, or are you off home?"

"I have five minutes, yes." She seated herself in front of his desk.

"I wanted a brief word about the garrotting on the moors. It's no surprise it's causing a stir with the media. The public are extremely concerned and the hospitality industry are applying pressure on the crime commissioner to do something about it, kick us up the backside and make us find this killer faster, basically. No surprises, but the crime commissioner is now after me."

"I know." Yvonne sighed. "All I can say is we are flat out, trying to catch him. I know you need leads ASAP, something to feed the press, and we're working on it. We have a few things in the pipeline, but it is too early to give any of what we have to the papers. I would suggest that campers stay away from the moors, for now. I am more concerned about saving lives than I am saving revenue for the tourist industry."

"They'll continue applying pressure on the council and the commissioner while they are losing money."

"I know. We will find this killer and the local campsites will recover. Hell, they may even get a flood of interest after everything that's happened. There are already more pages dedicated to the area online because of the link to the mysterious cave discovered by the first victim. Everyone wants to find the cave that made his body shake. I don't think the campsites will suffer for long, far from it. I think they will bounce back."

"I'm afraid they see it differently."

She cleared her throat, clenching and unclenching her fists. "I understand their frustration. All I can say is that myself and my officers are working our asses off on this." She glanced at the clock. "People are making considerable personal sacrifices to move this case forward. I will not push them harder than they are already pushing themselves. Now, if you don't mind, sir, I came to say goodnight and to say that I am finally going home, after a twelve-hour shift with only one twenty-minute break." She rubbed her eyes.

He nodded, his gaze softening. "Goodnight, Yvonne. Get some rest. You need it. Tomorrow is another day"

13

FISSURES

Yvonne could barely keep her eyes open on the drive home.

The sun having not yet crept behind the hills; she pulled over for five minutes, getting out for fresh air, drawing it deep into her lungs. The last thing she needed was to fall asleep at the wheel. Long hours and fitful sleeps were taking their toll.

She felt for Tasha. The psychologist had been putting up with her tossing and turning night after night.

When finally reaching home, the DI smiled, pulling into the drive. Thank goodness for her partner waiting inside to greet her. She would give her extra cuddles tonight.

Tasha had settled on the couch with a glass of chardonnay when Yvonne got in. She jumped up to help with the DI's coat and warm her dinner in the microwave.

"Tasha, I am so sorry I am this late back. It's hectic at the moment. The inquiry-"

"It's okay." Tasha held her. "You're in the middle of a murder investigation. You need not apologise and, least of all, to me."

"Thank you. I knew you would understand. I've been so looking forward to seeing you. I don't know what I would do, were you not here to greet me in the evenings. You are the best partner in the world."

Tasha bit her lip, her thoughts turning to London and the upcoming work for the Met. How could she tell Yvonne about this now?

"Tasha?" Yvonne pulled back to look into the psychologist's eyes. "Is something wrong?"

"No..." Tasha shook her head. "Everything is fine. Come on through and have something to eat. Shower, if you like. I'll have your food on the table for when you finish."

The DI rewarded her with a wide smile, "You are the best." She threw her arms around her one last time, before leaving for the shower.

True to her word, Tasha had a plate of pasta and salad waiting for Yvonne when she resurfaced in her dressing gown, with a towel around her head.

"Wow." Yvonne's red eyes regained some of their sparkle as she took her seat at the table. "I didn't realise how hungry I was."

"Good, eat, lady."

The DI tucked in, her eyes occasionally straying to the candle flames, allowing thoughts to come and go at will, washing over her fatigued brain, making no attempt to keep any of it. It was good to be home with the woman she loved.

"Penny for them?" Tasha stared at her, head inclined.

"I wasn't thinking of anything specific, only that it is good to be with you."

Tasha grimaced.

"There is something, isn't there? What is troubling you?" Yvonne placed her hand over her partner's. "Talk to me, please."

"I have to go away again, Yvonne. London."

"Another investigation with the Met?"

"Yes, I mean, I don't have to take it-"

"Hey..." The DI shook her head. "You must, Tasha. It is your work, and it is every bit as important as mine. I know, firsthand, how valuable your input is. You must go. I will miss you like crazy every moment you are away, but I understand and support you. Okay?"

Her partner smiled, her eyes watery as her thoughts turned to the tiny box. Now was not the time to proffer it. "Thank you for understanding. I love you," she said, her voice soft.

The DI slipped her arm around her waist. "I love you, too."

THE TEAM ARRIVED at the fissure they intended to explore. It was one of the still-uncharted tunnels that might require some excavation as they progressed. If this involved more than their portable shovels could manage, they would double back and look for another way in. They didn't have the equipment for large boulder removal, and safety had to be their highest priority.

As always, Ben led the team, with Brian bringing up the rear. Diane was in the number two position.

"Is everyone ready?" Ben asked, switching on his headlamp. "Gear sorted? Everybody's lights working?"

They each gave affirmation.

"Okay, let's go."

To access the opening, they had waded through a narrow tributary to the River Elwy.

The tunnel mouth was in a rock containing multiple

horizontal and vertical splits. They were entering one of the larger of the unexplored entry points.

The team were aware there could be rock falls inside and had agreed to take it steady.

They carried removable fluorescent tape they could use to mark the cave walls. Brian would be the only one to use it, unless they became separated. They each had their own colour, so other members of the team and rescuers could find them. It was an excellent system and had helped them out of trouble previously.

The series of tunnels, one of which they were about to explore, interconnected and formed part of a warren of unexplored passages inside the mountain. The chances of getting lost were high. The trick was to minimise that risk.

Ben hauled himself into the opening in the eastern bank of the gorge, helped by the other members of the team hoisting him up. The narrow tunnel stretched onward for about two metres, requiring a belly crawl, which he began by manoeuvring himself into position, then pushing with his knees and feet and grasping with his hands.

Puddles of water littered the rock floor and, as it also dripped from above, he was glad of his neoprene suit. The modern material was a godsend in wet conditions. He marvelled at the Victorian cavers who had coped without it.

After two-and-a-half metres, the tunnel widened, but began a gradual descent.

He could hear the others behind him, their movements amplified by the walls. He signalled that it was okay for them to follow, before moving on, his headlamp reflecting on cream rock, riddled with orange striations. The descending tunnel opened into a small chamber, no more than three metres square.

They would need their rope ladder to descend to the next level. The air was now perceptibly cooler.

Ben hammered bolts into the rock, adding carabiners, before attaching the rope ladder and testing for stability. He waited until everybody was together, before descending.

"I'll go as far as I can," he said to Diane. "I think the ladder is on the rock floor below, but I'll shout up to confirm."

"Got you," she acknowledged.

It had reached the bottom with several rungs to spare. They each carried a ladder in their packs, ensuring they had four available for every trip. If they ever needed more, they abandoned the expedition.

Brian, at the rear of the group, was already leaving the odd patch of marker tape, even though they had yet to meet any branches in the tunnel. With the possibility of their GPS failing, rescue services could still locate them, as he had also marked up the entrance they had used. Tunnel collapses were always a threat. It was always best to leave nothing to chance.

They had informed their spouses of where they would be, and their GPS had registered in the gorge. Here, however, deep in the bowels of the rock, they might have no signal. Brasgyll caves were notorious for having many black spots.

14

PROGRESS

Callum placed a file on the DI's desk, along with a cup of tea.

Full to the brim, she spilled some down her front. "Thank you, Callum," she said, brushing herself off. "What's in the file?"

"It's the forensic report for Gareth Sheldon. They confirmed the Garrotte as being a Fante's cheese wire, they estimate the perp to be the same build as the murderer of Mark Turner, and they got a DNA profile from the skin under one of Gary's nails they believe could be the killer. There is a lot in the report, ma'am, but that's my basic summary."

"We have the perpetrator's DNA? That is fantastic." She straightened her back. "So, Gary Sheldon scratched the killer's face... incredible."

"He may have the last word on his murderer."

"Thank goodness he got a nail on him."

"They confirmed it is a male profile, but it is not in the database, so the perp is not known to police."

"Okay, thank you, Callum. That is a super start. We

know Gary put up a fight. Maybe he left visible marks on the killer. Keep your eyes peeled when looking at suspects."

"Yes, ma'am."

As Callum returned to his desk, Yvonne mulled their second victim's murder. She was sure his resistance would have angered the killer. That, and the heated online discussions they'd had. Perhaps that explained the senseless trashing of Gary's belongings.

Their perp seemed a vengeful character, but Yvonne felt there was more to it. The murderer had gone to considerable trouble. If there was another purpose to these killings, they had yet to discover what that was.

He parked his four-by-four some distance from the gorge, planning to hike on foot, following the stream. It would bring him to the caves without leaving scent for police dogs.

He knew the group marked their entrances, he'd looked them up. They were meticulous. A close-knit team. They left nothing to chance. This would be his toughest challenge to date.

The water was up to his knees in places but, in waterproofs, he had no trouble making his way.

He could see the holes in the rock that served as entrances. It wouldn't take long to find the right one.

He donned his helmet and lamp from his backpack, leaving the rest of the gear until he was at the tunnel mouth. They would have prepared the way. Done all the hard work. If the tunnel proved blocked, and they met him on their way back, he wouldn't worry. They didn't know who he was. He looked like any other spelunker.

He was close, now. He scanned the holes above him. Where was it? A moment of doubt. Perhaps they hadn't left a marker at this one. He spotted the orange tape several feet above him and sighed with relief.

The height made climbing necessary. He heaved a boulder underneath. With the head-start, he could haul himself up through the access and into the crawl space. Grunting, he began the push through the tunnel.

15

FOUL PLAY

"Dai has there been any news regarding the extortion case that Mark Turner was showing interest in? Have fraud squad been back to us?"

Dai nodded. "They have, ma'am. They haven't caught the perp, yet. They are still wading through firewalls, and misdirected traces, and are not hopeful of a quick resolution. Sorry it's not better news, Yvonne."

"That's all right. Keep chasing it up for me, okay?"

"Will do, ma'am."

"Thought you might need these." Dewi plopped a mug and two chocolate digestives onto her desk.

"Oh, Dewi, you are a saint." She grinned. "How are you getting on with social media? Any ideas about the identity of Pierre Gram? Is he real or using a false name? We know he communicated with both of our victims and, since his personal information does not check out, we need an identity ASAP."

"I am almost certain he is operating under a false name, ma'am. It wouldn't be uncommon for social media, but as for his true identity?" He shrugged. "I hope to have his IP address soon, but he is hiding behind firewalls, and he may even use someone else's devices. It could take a while."

Yvonne pursed her lips. "I know, Dewi. I'm just concerned we may not have much time before he kills again. Please keep a close eye on who he's communicating with. Keep me informed. If he pays particular attention to anyone, especially if he is trolling them, I want to know about it."

"Yes, ma'am, I'll keep watching."

"That's great. Thank you, Dewi. And thank you for the tea and biscuits."

THEY HAD DROPPED *a ladder down the descent. He knew many of these tunnels had steep inclines and drops, forged by water. He smiled to himself. "Perfect," he whispered, unhooking the ladder from the carabiners, allowing it to fall into the blackness below. The wooden rungs clacked together as they hit the bottom, the sound echoing back up towards him.*

When he emerged through the entrance into the open, above the stream, he smirked.

The team of four was as good as buried. He took two breaths of the fresh air, sucking them deep into his lungs. It could be some time before those cavers got to do the same.

THE TEAM HAD ENTERED a tunnel with a shallow incline and only room enough to crawl.

Ben estimated they were now some thirty metres into the mountain. He called to the others to stop. A major collapse had filled the tunnel with soil and boulders of various sizes.

He examined the blockage with his torch. Some of it, he believed, they could remove with portable shovels and bare hands. However, some debris was too large to move, especially given the limited room they had to move around.

To his left, a tiny stream of water trickled in the opposite direction. Ben guessed water erosion had caused the collapse.

He shook his head. "We will not get through this, guys, we have to turn back."

Brian's heart sank. Bringing up the rear, he had witnessed Diane shaking from the cold and damp. The blockage couldn't have been more than ten metres from the other side of the mountain. They could have been out of there in under an hour.

As it was, they were now in for the long haul back, much of it uphill. And, without the chance of warming up, Brian feared his team mate's condition might deteriorate.

"Diane? How are you feeling?" He called to her.

"I'm good," she replied, her voice shaky.

"Do you need to stop?"

"No, let's keep going."

She was putting a brave face on. He knew this, but decided it best they press on, anyway. Keep her moving.

Disappointment rendered the crawl back more difficult mentally than it had been going forward.

Brian did his best to keep up a decent pace to get them back quickly and safely. They had been inside the mountain for approaching six hours, when the paramedic discovered their rope ladder lying in a crumpled heap on the floor of the vertical shaft. "What the blazes?" He picked it up, checking it over for an explanation of its failure. He could find none. The ladder was intact.

Next, he searched for the iron bolts and carabiners

which Ben had driven into the rock face. Perhaps they had worked themselves loose when they climbed down. They had not fallen and were therefore not the reason their ladder lay useless.

As the others joined him in the chamber, they realised with horror the seriousness of the situation. There was now no way out.

"I'll check our GPS." Ben pulled out a small, yellow box. "I'll alert rescue services."

He shook it, frowning. Fighting an urge to vomit, sweat beading on his upper lip, heart racing. "I can't get a signal," he said, holding the box in various positions over his head.

"How the hell did the ladder fall?" Diane asked, shivering.

"I think someone unhooked it." Brian's eyes met those of Ben.

"Sabotage? Surely not?" Ben took off his helmet to run a hand through his hair. "Who would do such a thing?"

"No-one would do this on purpose." Tim sat back on his heels. "Would they? And if they did, why?"

As their predicament sank in, the group fell silent.

Ben continued trying to get a signal for the GPS, to no avail. "Let's think about this." he said, taking his pack off his back. "There has to be a way out of here. We just need to think of it."

GRIM REAPER

Her sergeant puffed up the stairs.

"Have you been running, Dewi?" She grinned at him, her face straightening when she saw the strain on his. "What is it?"

"I've got a terrible feeling about this guy." He passed her the latest transcript of Pierre Gram's conversations. "Whoever he is, he is constantly trolling and goading other cavers. I think he is utilising psychological methods to agitate them and get them to reveal details such as plans for their next trips."

"I thought he would be."

"We know he goaded both Mark Turner and Gary Sheldon."

"Who is he working on now, Dewi?" Deep lines creased the DI's forehead. "What's he up to?"

"He's onto another group, a team of cavers from around Powys." Her sergeant pointed to the transcripts. "They are Ben Phillips, Brian Taylor, Diane Metcalfe, and Tim Wilson. They've been dealing with his comments well, to date, but they have been too open about their whereabouts. I think they have unwittingly put themselves in danger."

"That's not good..." She ran a hand through her hair.

"There's something else."

"Yes?"

"Well, it's just a thought, but Pierre Gram is an anagram of Grim Reaper. Coincidence?" Dewi searched her face. "What do you think?"

"So it is, Dewi, I think you could be on to something. We know his details are false. Why shouldn't his name be an anagram? It would fit with his personality. Brilliant work, Dewi."

"I wouldn't put anything past him."

"Can you do me a favour? Find out what trips that group of cavers have planned for the near future. Contact them and find out if they are okay. Warn them to be more circumspect about their upcoming excursions for the moment. Can you do that?"

"Yes, I'll get onto it this morning."

"Great. Let me know what they say. Also, find out if the social media sites can supply us with anything else which could identify this guy. See if they can help our tech guys with a trace. I want to know if we can get behind these firewalls."

"Yes, ma'am."

He can't hide forever. We will find him. Pray God, it is before he kills again."

"WILL we make it out of here?" Diane asked.

Brian noted her ashen face. "Yes, yes, of course we will.

We can do this. People know we are in this cave system. Rescuers will find us."

Ben nodded. "In the meantime, I think I will head back in and see if I can do anything about the tunnel blockage. See if I can make a crawl space through. Some boulders may be movable with care."

"I'll come with you." Tim moved towards Ben. "We'll do it together."

Ben checked with Brian. "Are you okay to stay with Diane? Rescuers are more likely to come in your end."

"I am." Brian pointed to Ben's pack. "Remember to use your tape. Mark your route."

"Will do." Ben and Tim set off, leaving Brian and Diane alone in the chamber.

Diane had ceased shivering, but her movements were slow and laboured, and she was blinking less. When she spoke, her words slurred. "It's so damp."

Brian pulled a foil blanket from his pack, wrapping it around her. "Keep this on," he said, sitting next to her. He could smell ketones on her breath. She was burning fat reserves. Hypothermia was setting in.

He grabbed a foil package from his rucksack. "We'll get some food down you. It will raise your blood sugar and warm you up."

"I have tea." Diane pulled out a flask from her pack. "We'll have some with the sandwiches."

Food and drink consumed, Brian noted the colour returning to his companion's cheeks. They had kept some sandwiches back, not knowing how long they would be underground. Brian sang, knowing he was tone deaf, but that the entertainment would elevate their spirits.

Diane was thankful for his presence. Grateful she wasn't

alone. The water running along the left side of the chamber, a thing of beauty, could also cause further rock collapses. It was pure, however, and they could drink it if needs be. She had the urge to nap and, although fighting to stay awake, within twenty minutes, she had given in.

17

THE CAVE

Callum got back to the DI with a likely location for Mark Turner's cave.

Dr Shearer had telephoned with GPS co-ordinates and emailed them relevant maps and charts.

Yvonne's eyes shone. "This is excellent, Callum. Let's get a team out there to look."

"He's pretty sure the cave will be an old mine."

"Yes, he told me, and he could well be right. After all, Turner's experience was in hiking, not caving. He would have struggled to tell the difference."

"I'll get in touch with uniform regarding a search team. They are likely to require community volunteers to help."

Yvonne nodded. "There may be local cavers who can provide support to officers, as long as they take care not to contaminate any crime scene. If they find the cave, Callum, I would like to know."

"Certainly, ma'am."

Yvonne leaned back in her chair and thought of Tasha. She was missing her. The house felt desolate without her.

She wondered if the psychologist was making progress

with the serial murder case in London. If she knew Tasha, that was a given. Cool under pressure. There wasn't much the psychologist could not achieve when she put her mind to it.

The DI felt that her partner was storing something up. Holding back. It wasn't anything the psychologist had said, more what she hadn't said, and the stiffness in her shoulders when discussions turned to personal matters.

Yvonne resolved to quiz her Tasha on her return.

THE SUN PELTED down from a clear sky.

On the moors, there was no relief. The DI was grateful of the forensic tents and took full advantage until they allowed her closer to the cave. A minor wood occupied the left side of the cleft in which it nestled. But this was subject to an ongoing search and was not available for shelter.

She swabbed the sweat from her brow before donning a protective suit and overshoes.

Just as Dr Shearer had predicted, the cave was an old mine entrance, thought to have been dug by the romans and excavated by the early Victorians. No documents existed for it. Though there were records for various shafts in the area, this one remained a mystery.

Yvonne pondered what Mark had said about the cave causing his body to vibrate and wondered whether she might feel similar tremors. There had been no earthquakes at the time he visited the cave, perhaps he was a sensitive individual who had picked up resonance from something.

As she exited the tent, she waited for the signal from SOCO to say she could enter the cave.

Instead, an officer approached her.

"You can go in," he said, pulling his mask away from his mouth.

She could see the perspiration on his upper lip. "Find anything?"

He nodded. "We found traces of blood and skin on the rock, which could fit with the abrasions on Turner's fingers. We should confirm whether the traces belong to him within the next forty-eight hours. Luminol showed blood in several locations. It must have taken several minutes for him to die. He struggled for his life."

Yvonne winced. She knew much of this already, but the officer's words brought the images to life, causing her heart to thump erratically, as though someone was about to garrotte her.

She turned towards the cave. "Thank you, I think I'll look for myself, now."

He nodded and stepped aside.

The entrance was narrow, requiring her to turn sideways. Once inside, however, it opened into a small chamber she could stand in without hitting her head. A passage exited to the back of the cavern. It required a crawl to get through the opening.

She wondered whether the original miners had kept the entrance small on purpose, keeping it hidden.

On the floor and walls, she could see the numbered markers left by SOCO, showing where they had found trace evidence.

Above her, tree roots hung from the roof, gnarled fingers reaching for her hair. Water dripped into small amber pools dotted around the chamber.

A grim place to die. She shuddered. She had to witness the crime scene for herself to better understand perpetrator and victim, but it left her nauseated.

The killer had lain in wait here for some time. What motivated him? Was it psychopathy? Or was there something else behind his pathological behaviour? Was there a reason for it?

She felt in her gut the answers lay in the social media posts of Pierre Gram, the Grim Reaper. The DI determined to find out who, or what, Pierre Gram was.

18

BRASGYLL GORGE

She arrived back in the office with no time to grab refreshment.

Dewi needed her. "Ma'am, you know those cavers from Powys I was telling you about?" He put his hands on his hips and sighed. "They're missing. Last known location, Brasgyll Gorge. Relatives expected them back yesterday evening, but they didn't show. No-one has contacted them, either via mobile, or on their GPS. There is an emergency beacon built into the team's GPS unit, but they haven't had a signal from it. North Wales Cave Rescue are on their way to the gorge, as we speak."

The DI frowned. "Why were they not called out last night?"

"Apparently, GPS signalling is hit-and-miss from several of the cave systems in the gorge, and delays in people getting back are a common occurrence. Cavers regularly get back late. The families raised the alarm because it has been nearly twenty-four hours since they were due home, and thirty-six hours since anyone heard from them."

She nodded. "Very well, Dewi. Where is Brasgyll Gorge?"

"It's on private land, off the River Elwy. The Cefn Estate."

"Was their location posted on social media?"

"It was, ma'am."

"I see. Can we get up there?"

"I can drive us there."

"Make sure North Wales know to have armed officers on hand, Dewi. We know this killer is dangerous, and we don't know where he is."

"Right you are. I'll get on to them."

As the DI turned away, her nausea had returned. This disappearance was too much of a coincidence, given the attention Pierre Gram had been paying the group. She hoped he wasn't at that gorge.

BEN PULLED at one of the larger rocks, manoeuvring himself such that Tim could get in closer to help.

The tight space made it difficult to get a purchase on the boulder and move it from its position. They had no chance of creating a large enough gap without removing the rock, but it was taking considerable time and energy to budge it even a short distance.

They moved it by about a foot, allowing them to clear the soil, shale and smaller rocks from the blockage.

They didn't know how deep the barrier was, but clearing some of it might give them a better idea.

Both men had folding shovels in their backpacks. They set to work, sweat building inside their neoprene suits.

While Brian and Diane were feeling the cold, Ben and

Tim were fighting the heat they were generating in such a confined space.

The older man checked his watch again. Time was moving on. The others would worry, and he and Tim were nowhere close to clearing a passage. It would get dark outside of the mountain. Their spouses would not raise the alarm until the morning. It would be the afternoon at the earliest before rescuers could get to them. Diane was not in good shape. They had to keep going.

It was hard work, but they removed the equivalent of three backpack's worth of soil and shale, spreading it out down the sides of the crawl space. It revealed more boulders, though thankfully not as large as the first.

Ben got a hold on one and teased it from the pile, realising too late that it had a pivotal stabilising role for the rest of the rubble.

Rock and shale tumbled towards them. Ben pulled back, attempting to grab Tim to get him out of the way.

The shale and rocks impacted both men, but an enormous boulder struck Tim, knocking him backwards.

Ben heard him groaning under the rubble. "Tim?" He crawled over, raising the rock enough to roll it off his friend. The impact had broken Tim's arm, and he had a two-inch gash on his temple.

The main first aid kit was with Brian, but Ben carried antiseptic wipes and bandages.

Taking out paracetamol and water, he first administered those, making sure Tim had swallowed, before bandaging his broken arm tight against his chest. Both Tim's radius and ulna appeared broken. Thankfully, there were no other injuries, aside from the gash to the forehead, to which Ben applied antiseptic, lint and a further bandage.

"You will be all right, mate," he reassured the groaning

casualty. "Try to keep that arm still. The pain killers should kick in before long and help a little." He took off his jacket, wrapping it around his friend's shoulders.

Heart heavy, he knew there would now be no way to dig themselves out of the mountain. Their only option was to make their way back to Brian and Diane, and they wouldn't be able to do that until Tim had taken some time to recover from the shock of his injury. Even then, getting back to the others would not be easy.

Ben felt his first pang of fear. The situation was becoming critical. With Tim as injured as he was, hypothermia would be a serious threat to him. Ben should get him moving as soon as possible.

DEWI PARKED the car in a lay-by, taking a few moments with Yvonne to gaze around at the undulating landscape. Hills, trees, rocks and water. The place had everything. A great environment to go walking, he thought. It had taken them two hours to get there. The chance to stretch their legs was a welcome one.

They were in Nant-Y-Graig, where the Brasgyll Caves were situated.

There were several other vehicles parked up, two of which were the four-by-fours of the North Wales Cave Rescue team.

The detectives headed for the flurry of activity in the gorge, steep rock faces rising on either side. They had informed North Wales police they would attend the rescue, and of the potential for there to be a killer in the gorge.

Uniformed officers from North Wales were in attendance, standing around until cave rescuers had investigated, and located the tunnel used by the cavers.

A team of specialist officers were donning safety gear further on. Yvonne approached one of them and introduced herself.

"You think we've got a killer on the loose, then?" He grinned, as though he doubted there was.

She didn't blame him. She might feel the same in his shoes, in such a peaceful place.

She smiled. "We don't know. We've had two murders in our area and our chief suspect has been paying this group a lot of interest online. He encourages other cavers to take risks they wouldn't otherwise. We think he lies in wait for them near, or at, the caves they explore."

"What does he do to them?"

"He garrottes them."

"I see." He wasn't smirking now. "God, I hope that's not why this group are missing. I hope they've gotten themselves lost."

Yvonne nodded. "I hope that, too, but I am afraid for them."

"Arwel." He offered her his hand. "Arwel Thomas. If this rescue requires police, I will lead the boys going in."

"Pleased to meet you. I am impressed North Wales have a caving team."

"Well, we are not officially a caving team within the police, but we are cavers who are police officers. The gear and the risk is our own."

"I hope you're not needed."

"So do I."

"Why are they standing around?" She pointed towards the red-suited rescue team."

He sighed. "They don't know which entrance the

cavers used. They have found no markers yet, and GPS signalling is poor in this region. So, they don't know where they are."

"They have a reputation for being thorough, and they always fluorescent markers." Yvonne frowned.

"Well," he said, staring at the rock face, "let's hope they find something soon."

The DI pursed her lips. "I don't like this. I don't like this one bit."

"You think your killer would travel this far?" He tilted his head, studying her face.

"I don't know but, if I'm honest? I wouldn't put anything past him. He's a careful planner, and I've a feeling he'll be enjoying this."

BRIAN KEPT Diane as warm as he could, cradling her and encouraging her to move around when necessary. He had so far stove off the worst effects of hypothermia. They had a few chocolate bars left between them, and there were sandwiches and biscuits left, along with tea in their flasks. The latter wouldn't stay warm forever.

There was no privacy. Each had already had to turn their backs while the other toileted.

Since Ben and Tim were still not back, they hoped the guys had achieved a breakthrough at the other end of the tunnel.

However, when the injured Tim and crestfallen Brian returned, it was clear, even before they spoke, their mission had failed. There would be no way out of the mountain until rescuers found them.

"I'm sorry." Ben shook his head. "We couldn't do it."

"What happened?" Brian asked, crossing to Tim to check him over.

"We had a rockfall." Ben shook his head. "It covered him. I think it broke both bones in his forearm."

Brian carefully examined Tim, as the latter moaned in pain. "It's broken. You're right, both bones, I think. Did you treat him for shock?" he asked, lifting both of the injured man's eyelids and shining a pen torch in them.

"I gave him water and paracetamol, and we rested for a while after I bandaged him. He's just taken two ibuprofen."

"Okay." Brian helped Tim to a more comfortable position, where the floor was more even, taking out another foil blanket to wrap around him. He took out a splint for the broken limb. "We'll soon have you feeling better," he said, placing a pulse oximeter on his finger.

"Is there anything I can do to help?" Diane asked, having perked up a little at the others' return.

"His obs are fine at the moment. You could sit with him, Di, keep each other warm."

She nodded. "I can do that."

Ben and Brian moved further away.

"How long do you think it'll be until rescuers arrive?" Brian asked, taking his helmet off and running a hand through his hair.

Ben shook his head. I don't know for sure, obviously, but they ought to be in the gorge already. I'm hoping our marker is still visible at the entrance."

"Oh God," Brian sighed, "It had better be."

"Let's hope so."

19

TENSION

A shout went up from the rescue team members.

"They've found the entrance, ma'am. The fluorescent markers were still there." Dewi rejoined her, having been talking with the rescuers.

"Thank God. Hopefully, they'll find them soon." She sighed, her shoulders lowered. "Why did it take so long?" She frowned.

"It seems they may have used an alternative entrance to their originally planned one, ma'am. Changed their minds about which tunnels they wanted to explore. It's definitely their marker. Brian Taylor's name is on it."

"Okay. Are the rescuers going in?" She nodded at the men in red, wondering why they weren't in there already.

"They are. Arwel Thomas is heading in with them, in case our killer is in there."

"Okay, good." Yvonne still felt nauseous. Something wasn't right. "Why would an experienced team of cavers change their entry point last minute?"

Dewi shrugged. Maybe they came across an unexpected rock fall? I don't know. I have little knowledge of caving."

"You're right. Presumably, they had their reasons." Ahead of her, the rescuers carried portable stretchers, ropes, carabiners, and other equipment into the mountain, led by Arwel.

The DI and her sergeant could only watch.

HE COULD SEE them in the gorge below, checking their gear, planning their course of action, barking orders.

He smirked. This would be interesting.

She piqued his curiosity as he adjusted his binoculars. The woman hanging back, running her hands through mussed blonde hair. There was something about her stance and the frown on her face. She had concerns. Smelled a rat. A police officer. What was she doing there? Police normally left this sort of thing to rescuers. So why was she there? Was she onto him?

He would find out, perhaps have a little sport.

The older man was back at her side. A subordinate, he could tell from their body language, though it was clear they had an easy, even friendly, relationship. The man appeared less tense than she. Perhaps time would change that.

And time would soon run out for those inside the mountain. It was cold down there. Trapped for almost forty-eight hours, it could be a further forty-eight before rescuers found them.

HER MOBILE RANG.

"Callum?" She put a hand over her other ear to better hear him. "Is everything okay?"

"Ma'am, I thought you should know the Pierre Gram has been active on social media."

She frowned into the phone. "How long?"

"Most of the day, on-and-off. He was on yesterday, too."

"Thanks, Callum. Keep a track of who he is contacting and let me know." She ended the call, turning to Dewi. "Well, the Grim Reaper can't be in there, he's been on Facebook. He wouldn't be able to do that from inside those caves."

"What do you want to do?"

"We'll phone through to North Wales, let them know, and head back to Newtown. I have a feeling that Pierre Gram is messing us about. I hope to God he hasn't led us up the garden path to get someone in Newtown while we are up here."

Dewi pointed back towards the gorge. "Let's hope not. Are we assuming those cavers are okay?"

"Well, they may not be, they are still somewhere in that mountain, but they are not likely to be murder victims. The best people are on the case, I think we can leave them to it. To be honest, there's not a lot we can do here, anyway. We have a double murder to solve."

"I'll drive." Dewi searched his pockets for the car keys. A moment of panic replaced by his shaking them in triumph. "Let's go."

20

SOMETHING AFOOT

Callum greeted them back at Newtown station, shirt sleeves rolled up. "He's targeting someone else."

"Really?" She raised her brows, throwing her jacket on the back of a chair. "Who?"

"Mark Turner's best friend, John Blackman."

"The maths teacher?" She put a hand to her forehead, clicking her tongue on the roof of her mouth. "God, no. He has a heavily pregnant wife. She is due any day."

"Should we warn him?" Dewi asked, filling the kettle.

"I don't know." Yvonne thought for a moment. "He won't be caving, or even thinking about it, not as it stands. He is making sure he is available if his wife goes into labour. So, I don't think there is an immediate danger."

"Okay." Dewi nodded.

"Callum, could you do me a favour? I meant to check that Blackman really has a pregnant wife. I have no reason to doubt his story, but would you mind confirming it for me?"

"Sure."

"If he is being goaded by Gram, then I may speak with him to make sure he doesn't go hiking, especially with his wife so close to giving birth. I'll contact North Wales later, find out how the rescue is progressing. I hope they bring those cavers out alive." She turned to Dewi. "Can you get me the transcripts of the conversation between Gram and Blackman?"

"I'll get them printed now, Yvonne."

"Good, let's see if we can predict his next move."

It was clear from the transcripts that Gram wanted Blackman to explore Mark Turner's cave, now that police had finished with it.

Blackman was not the only one on Gram's radar, but he seemed to pay most attention to him, perhaps because the maths teacher had been too vocal in his support of his friend, Mark.

Yvonne resolved to speak with Blackman and warn him of the dangers of going into the cave. She had to do so carefully, not wanting to compromise the case.

He agreed to see her in his free period again, as he didn't want his wife more worried than she already was, since Mark's death.

"Why do I feel this is unpleasant news?" he asked.

She accepted the chair he offered. "I wouldn't say it was unpleasant news but you ought to be vigilant. I would suggest steering clear of hiking or caving."

"Why?" His eyes narrowed.

The world outside had greyed-out with the drizzle that fell from a darkened sky.

"We think Mark's killer encouraged him to go to that

cave. So, no matter what you feel tempted to do, I would advise against adventuring, and especially not on your own."

"Do you know who it was?" he asked, eyes wide. "Is my wife in danger? My unborn child?"

Yvonne shook her head. "I cannot say for sure, obviously, but I think the risk is more to yourself, if you hike or explore alone in the country. But, like I say, it would be wise to stay vigilant, wherever you are."

"Understood. I'm not sure I feel reassured, without knowing who it is I need to be wary of." Deep furrows lined his forehead.

"I am not at liberty to name anyone, at this stage, and we do not know for certain who the killer is, but pay attention to anyone intent on arguing with you. They may encourage you to explore that cave, now its location is public knowledge. I can't say any more than that."

"Got it." He nodded. "Thank you for letting me know."

She smiled, allowing her gaze to wander the tiny office-come-tearoom. "Do you always have coffee alone?"

He shook his head. "Not always, sometimes one or other of my colleagues join me. But, often, it is just myself."

She pursed her lips, saying nothing.

"I could go to the main staffroom, if I chose, but it's more convenient here, just across the corridor from my classroom. Why travel? Especially in this weather."

"You have a point. It must get lonely though, having tea by yourself?"

"Not really, I do my planning in here." He pointed to a shelf containing several files. "I can easily find enough to occupy me." He tilted his head. "Was there something else?"

"We still don't have a motive for Mark's murder."

"I see. And now, there has been a second murder."

Blackman folded his arms. "Aren't we looking at a serial killer?"

She shook her head. "We can't say that, unless he kills again, but I wouldn't rule it out, either. This could be the work of a psychopath. We are investigating two murders. That is enough to be going on with. Remember what I said about not going on excursions. We wouldn't want you to be the reason we are looking for a serial killer."

He nodded. "I'll stay home."

Yvonne telephoned North Wales.

A desk sergeant brought her up to speed. "It's not going well. The rescue team are getting tired and desperate. They followed the fluorescent markers into the mountain for several hours until there were no more pieces of tape. No sign of the cavers. They have now begun splitting up into teams of two or three and trying various tunnels into the mountain."

"Oh, no..." Yvonne sighed.

"Yes, they will have to keep trying until they find the right one."

"I wouldn't want to be those explorers, stuck in there for what may be yet another night."

"Neither would I and, if there are casualties... Well, it doesn't bear thinking about."

"No wonder it exhausted the rescue team. They won't have rested." As the DI ended the call, she wondered if someone had moved the cavers' markers to the wrong tunnel system. Someone would have to get to the bottom of what had happened, and fast.

HOPE OR DESPERATION

Inside the mountain, the team of four finished the last of their sandwiches. They had two chocolate bars left between them. After that, all food would be gone.

They had consumed the tea whilst it could still confer heat. That left five small bottles of water.

Now and then, Ben would raise his hand, signalling the others to maintain silence, while they listened for noise. If they heard rescuers, they could bang their metal mugs and hammers on the walls, and shout for attention. So far, there had been nothing, save for the trickle of the water which flowed through the left-hand side of the chamber.

Between the silences, they sang and told stories to keep their spirits up, spinning an empty bottle to decide whose turn it was to go next. Despite this, each minute stretched to fantastic proportions. Time was an expansile entity in these tunnels.

Ben imagined that, for the rescuers, the opposite must be true. A feeling that time went too fast, like something shrunk in the wash, but at least they could make progress, unlike themselves.

He looked around at his brave friends. Tim and Diane were in the worst shape physically but, mentally, they were all struggling.

This was where his considerable experience would be most useful. He had twice before needed rescue. He related the stories to his friends.

"The first time, I was only twenty-two, and had fallen down a twelve-foot drop, breaking my ankle on an expedition in Nidderdale, Yorkshire. That time, I spent only six hours underground, waiting for rescue. It was no fun being in pain, but boy was I relieved to see those headlamps coming in my direction, I can tell you."

"It must have been frightening." Diane said, as she and the others hearkened, glad of the distraction.

"The second time, I was thirty, and had gotten lost in a cave network at Alderley Edge, in the Peak District. It took almost twenty-four hours for them to get to us then. I have to say, this is the longest I have ever been underground, and has been the toughest, but I am confident help will come. We will get out of this."

As he said the words, Ben knew that nearly one hundred and fifty cavers had lost their lives in the UK. Around ten of those bodies had never recovered. He didn't believe they were in any danger of death, but that could change for many reasons, such as an unexpected downpour flooding the system or hypothermia, if rescuers couldn't find them. However, it would do no-one any good for him to dwell.

Yvonne watched the conversation develop.

Pierre Gram was up to his trolling tricks.

She noticed how he stayed just the right side of nasty. He

mixed his messages, praising people's skills, one moment, then telling them why a certain action might be impossible, the next. He drew them in, involving them in the conversation despite themselves. He worked the discussion the way she imagined he might work a room.

John Blackman was one of those involved in the chat.

Gram was explaining how exploring Mark Turner's cave and subsequent tunnel system would gain someone instant fame on YouTube and Facebook cavers' pages. "Think of the subscribers," he typed. "All that extra revenue for your new baby when it arrives."

The DI got the impression Blackman was thinking about that. His answer was slow in coming. Surely Gram hadn't tempted him? Not after she explained the dangers to the maths teacher?

When he replied, it confirmed her worst fears. "You have a point there," he wrote. "It probably wouldn't take more than a few hours to complete a reconnaissance trip to the tunnel. I could drive up there, shorten the time it takes as much as possible."

"I could come with you," another male, Todd Garrett, added. "I am dying to see it, and the police recommend not going up there alone. Going together would be the perfect solution."

Yvonne clicked on Garrett's personal details. If they were correct, he was twenty-four and had been into spelaeology, the technical name for potholing, for five years.

She wondered what Gram would make of Garrett going with Blackman. If Pierre was the killer, would it put him off trying to attack them? Or would he strike, anyway?

Whichever, she didn't intend taking chances. Her team and specialist officers would monitor that cave throughout, from the day before the planned exploration, to the end. If the Grim Reaper attended, he would be in for a nasty shock.

She called Dewi over. "This could be it. Our chance to catch the killer, Gram, if he is our psychopath."

"What's happening?" He asked, leaning over her shoulder.

She filled him in with the conversation and pointed to Blackman's latest answer as he typed it. "Blackman is going to the cave, Dewi. He is going against our advice, and he is taking a younger man with him."

"They are going to the cave?" Her sergeant grimaced. "We should stop them."

Yvonne nodded. "Perhaps, but I already advised Blackman against it. They are adults, Dewi. We set up water-tight surveillance and catch Gram, or whoever is our killer, in the attempt."

He shook his head. "Yvonne, it's not like you to take risks like this. What if he harms them?"

"I know what you are saying, Dewi. We could undertake surveillance from twelve hours before Blackman and Garrett arrive. Our killer would be unlikely to lie in wait for longer than that. Plus, we'll get specialist officers to check the tunnel, ensure it is clear. We can continue to watch and monitor as they arrive and while they are in there. If Gram turns up, we go after him and catch him. We can follow anyone who turns up, because they are likely to be Gram. We can arrest on suspicion and get a DNA sample. If he is our killer, we can compare his DNA with SOCO's profile of the perp. If we have a match, job done. We'll obviously have to keep a low profile, stay some distance back. We can use the trees and hedgerow as cover and have cameras close to the cave entrance and inside the cave and tunnel. We'll know and capture everything going on."

Dewi nodded. "Sounds a pretty solid plan and, if we have throughly checked beforehand, and set up cameras, that makes me a lot happier about it. We should still run this past his nibs."

Yvonne grinned. "Leave the DCI to me. It looks like Blackman is planning it for next Saturday. Get onto the dive team, see of they have cavers amongst them, officers that can do the reccy for us and set up the camera surveillance. If we know what is available, it will help me persuade Llewelyn."

"Should we have armed officers on standby?" Dewi tilted his head. "In case it all kicks off? We know he carries a garrotte. What we don't know is if he carries other weapons."

"Yes, I think we should have armed officers up there. I'll speak to the DCI."

"Good luck, it's resource intensive with no guarantee of a result. He will not be happy."

She shrugged. "It wouldn't be the first time we have flown by the seat of our pants, Dewi. I believe we will get the result."

Her sergeant sighed. "Let's hope you're right."

22

MAKING HEADWAY

The SOCO report confirmed the blood traces found in the cave belonged to Mark Turner.

They had also repeated the tests confirming the perp's DNA profile sequenced from Gary Sheldon's nails.

The news thrilled Yvonne. If they caught Pierre Gram going to the Dolfor Moors cave, they could arrest him on suspicion and have grounds for a DNA sample.

A lot rested on the surveillance being bullet proof. They would need to keep everything tight and follow procedure rigorously.

Callum and Dai had been working their way through the members of that Facebook group, and Pierre Gram still stood out as the most likely perpetrator. No-one else appeared to be hiding their identity and using so many firewalls.

Yvonne was positive they were on the right track.

BEN HELD UP HIS HAND. "Wait, what was that?" he called to the others.

They held their collective breath, listening for the sounds he had witnessed.

"There!" Diane tapped Brian on the arm.

"I heard it." Brian nodded. "Quick, bang the walls."

They used their hammers and metal mugs, banging for all they were worth on the rock face, and shouting until their throats hurt. The fact there was no ladder down to their position could cause rescuers to turn back if they didn't hear them.

"Hold it." Ben held his hand up once more.

"Hello? Is anybody down there?"

The group thought they had never heard such a wonderful sound. They shouted and cheered and banged. There was no chance of anyone getting away without hearing them.

A tear of relief tracked its way down the team leader's face. Thank heaven for the cave rescue team.

"Anyone injured down there?"

"One injured." Ben instructed.

Diane and Brian hugged each other as Ben crossed to Tim to help him prepare for being hoisted up first. A red-suited rescuer dropped on the winch with a stretcher. The site of his boots appearing from above generated another cheer from the group.

"You are a sight for sore eyes, mate." Brian shook the man's hand. "We were losing hope."

When a second rescuer dropped into the chamber, they strapped Tim into the stretcher and pulled on the rope to signal those above to hoist him up.

They provided a rope ladder for the others.

Finally, they were on their way to freedom.

23

BARRIERS

Yvonne knocked on the DCI's door, going straight in. She didn't have time for etiquette. The clock was ticking, and she needed to know they could have everything in place for their operation.

The DCI's support would be vital to get the specialist help they required, including armed response and, if needed, the helicopter. If they had to go in, the DI wanted it hard and fast. There would be no room for error.

She glanced at the paperwork stacked high on his desk, hoping her request would take priority.

"Yvonne." Both his eyebrows raised. "What is it? You look like someone on a mission."

"I am, sir. I need your permission to carry out a surveillance and capture operation at the Dolfor Moors cave."

He frowned, running a hand through the top of his hair. "Since when have you needed my permission to carry out surveillance? It's bread and butter-"

"It's not just the watching, it's the circumstances." She

explained what they needed, and why. "There could be serious consequences if it goes wrong."

He shook his head. "I'm not sure I can sanction it, Yvonne."

She explained how they planned to ensure the cavers' safety and catch the suspect.

He listened, head tilted, rubbing his chin and sighing, periodically. "I see... Look, leave it with me. I will liaise with the other departments. If we can get everything we need for the operation, then... maybe. I will get back to you as soon as possible, okay?"

Yvonne closed his door, knowing she would spend the day on tenterhooks until he got back to her.

Wiping sweaty palms on her skirt, she headed back to the office. Social media waited for no woman. If Blackman and Garrett delayed their trip, she needed to know sooner rather than later.

IT WASN'T until her arrival home at just before nine o'clock that night; she allowed herself to relax.

She did so with a long, frosty glass of rioja, a change from the chardonnay she would normally choose.

After showering, she donned PJs, sipped her wine, and took a fish pie portion from the freezer, putting it in the microwave. She knew how good it would taste. It was one of Tasha's, leftover after they had both eaten generous portions of it, freshly baked.

She smiled to herself at this connection with her partner and wondered how the psychologist was getting on in her case with the Met.

As if she could read her mind, the phone rang. Her partner's gentle tones graced the other end.

"Tasha!" Yvonne did not hide her excitement.

"Well, that is a wonderfully happy greeting. I think somebody is missing me?" She chuckled.

"You bloody know I am." Yvonne laughed. "I was only musing how great it is that I can eat your lovingly created food even when you are not here. How is it going in London?" She settled herself on the sofa, sipping her wine, the fish pie still warming in the microwave.

"We are getting on well, Yvonne. I have furnished them with a profile I am happy with, and they tell me they have a strong suspect already. I am hoping this means I will be back with you before too long."

The DI smiled into the phone. "Tasha that is fantastic news. I am so pleased. I hope you are right and that you are back here soon. I really am missing you. We are reaching a critical period in our murder case too, I feel. We are carrying out surveillance on Saturday, and hope to have our perp in the bag by Saturday night."

The DI could sense her partner frowning on the other end.

"You're not doing anything dangerous are you?"

Yvonne laughed. "No, why would I do that?"

"I know what you're like. I'm serious. Do not do anything dangerous. I swear I will come there now."

"Don't do that, Tasha. I am teasing. I will not be putting myself in harm's way."

"Good." Tasha's voice softened. "I want you in one piece when I get back, DI Giles."

"And I shall be, Dr Phillips." Yvonne grinned. "I shall be."

There was an uncharacteristic pause on the other end.

"Tasha? Are you okay? Was there something else?" she asked, holding her breath. Another pause. "Nothing else, Yvonne. Sleep well tonight." And the psychologist had gone.

Yvonne frowned as she set down her phone. What was up with Tasha?

~

THE FOLLOWING morning saw the DI on the phone with North Wales police, affirming that the cave rescue had been successful, with no loss of life.

Yvonne fist-pumped the air. "Thank God, well done to your officers and the rescue team," she said to DI Griffiths on the other end.

"Thank you," he answered, his voice gruff. "Someone switched their marker tape from the tunnels they were in to other tunnels." He clicked his tongue. "It looks like the perp followed them to the gorge and moved it to confuse everybody."

"Really?"

"Yes. We think the same person removed their rope ladder and threw it down the vertical shaft to trap them in the mountain. Without rescue they wouldn't have gotten out as there had been a serious rock fall and collapse, near the exit, on the opposite side of the mountain."

"Thank God they told people where they would be."

He grunted. "It still took nearly forty-eight hours to locate and get them out of there."

"Whoever did it, knew their actions could cause four deaths." Yvonne pressed her lips together.

"Exactly. I am thinking, perhaps, your killer followed them to the gorge."

"Maybe, he watched us all for a while." The DI sighed. "Our killer is a nasty piece of work."

As she put down the phone, Yvonne thought of Pierre Gram, even more sure that the Grim Reaper would turn up on Saturday. Well, let him. She would be waiting.

24

A STRANGE DISEASE

"He had Myasthaenia Gravis, your victim, Mark Turner."

Yvonne tilted her head, staring at Hanson, as the pathologist donned his coat, ready to leave the mortuary for the day.

"What does that mean?" she asked, blinking as she took this additional fact on board.

"It's a neuromuscular condition. The body produces antibodies against its own acetylcholine receptors."

"I see." She didn't.

"It causes muscle weakness, most often starting in the facial muscles and spreading to other parts of the body. It can affect anywhere."

"And Mark Turner had it?"

Hanson nodded. "He hadn't seen doctors about it. It was undiagnosed. When you told me he had felt tremors in his body while he was at the cave, I wondered if he might have had a medical condition that explained it. I took bloods and sent them for testing. The tests for multiple sclerosis came back negative. On the off-chance, I sent samples to Oxford

Neurosciences Department for them to test for Myasthaenia. The result was positive. He was in the early stages of the disease and, unusually, it was affecting his trunk muscles."

"So, the cave experience, the tremors that was a coincidence?"

Hanson nodded. "Perhaps, but symptoms can appear or worsen with stress. Finding the cave could have brought on symptoms."

"The cave didn't make him shake then, his condition did."

"Absolutely."

"What would have happened if he had continued to live? Would he have lost the ability to hike? Walk, even?"

"Not necessarily, but it was a possibility, yes. There is no cure as yet. Occasionally the condition gets better by itself, but that is rare. Treatments can slow disease progression or lessen symptoms, as can rest. But, eventually, he probably wouldn't have been hiking much. At its worst, it causes respiratory failure because of damage to the respiratory muscles."

"I see. Thank you, Roger." The DI cast her eyes around the white mortuary, with its washed and shiny metal surfaces and smell of disinfectant. Miracles happened here. The dead had a voice.

As they left, Hanson switched off the lights. "You're welcome."

The DI pondered the disease as she got into her car.

Mark Turner had been murdered because of the symptoms of a debilitating condition. His explanation of them angered a psychopath.

It would have been natural for Turner, an athletic and outgoing youthful man, to assign his strange symptoms to an external rather than an internal cause. Who wouldn't in the same circumstances?

Her heart went out to him and his family. It made her even more determined to bag his killer.

HE CHECKED HIS KIT. Helmet, lamp, spare batteries, pads, wet weather gear. Garrottes.

He was ready.

Timing was everything. If he got this right, it would be quick. Noiseless. Almost.

The trick was to make sure the victim was unaware until the last moment, when he could do nothing about it. And he was becoming practised. The second murder had been easier than the first.

He took a sip from his beer. Planning was hard work, especially in this heat.

He watched condensation snake its way down the bottle. That was one thing about caves. Their temperature. No matter what the weather was doing, caves kept their cool and cleared his head. Heat turned thoughts into less than useful things. And he needed clarity. The success of his plans depended on it.

25

NIGGLING DOUBT

The morning briefing had them all sleeves rolled up, notepads at the ready, and focussed.

Yvonne cast her eyes over each of their faces, filled once more with pride. Everyone of them wanted this killer caught. Whatever it took.

"There's something that's been bothering me." She pursed her lips. "We have two murders in this area, then our suspected killer goads a team of cavers online, and follows them to a cave system in North Wales, we think. What he does next makes no sense."

"Because he doesn't kill them?" Callum called out.

"Yes precisely, that. He doesn't kill them. If Pierre Gram is our killer, there is a lot more to this than meets the eye. My personal suspicion is that he had no intention of killing them. He travels up north, follows them to the cave, moves their tape, throws their ladders down, and causes a lot of frustration. He does all that, but he knows we will rescue them. So why do it? Why go to all that trouble to set something up and not follow through. What was he doing?"

"Do you think he's toying with us?" Dewi asked, hands on hips.

"I think that is a possibility, yes. Don't you? What if he was still up at that gorge, the entire time, watching the police operation, and revelling in it? Manipulating us just as much as he had manipulated the cavers."

"But, why?" Dai asked, his pen tucked behind his ear.

Yvonne tilted her head. "Well, perhaps, there we get into his motivation for the murders. There is something more to this. If we assume that the apparent attempted murder of the caving team was a red herring, then we come back to our two local murders."

Callum frowned. "I think it's a stretch to assume he wasn't intending to harm those cavers. It would have been too easy for them to have suffered injury or death in that situation."

"I'm not saying he didn't intend them harm, Callum. To be honest, I don't think he really cared about the outcome for them. One way or the other, they served their purpose whether they lived or died. It makes us believe that we are looking for a travelling serial killer. But we have a fair amount of experience, now, of going after serial killers. They are meticulous. They leave very little to chance. I believe that if he wanted those cavers dead, they would be."

She continued. "That tells me he did not want them dead or, more likely, he didn't bother to go to the trouble of killing them because they had already served their purpose, looking like intended victims."

"Are you saying we are not dealing with a true serial killer?" Dai asked.

"That is what I am thinking, yes."

"So, what are we dealing with?"

"Well, I keep coming back to our first victim, Mark

Turner, and his file of newspaper cuttings. Why was he so interested in those fraud cases? I want you to go through his finances again. I know we've gone over them and found nothing untoward, but could there be other accounts we haven't found yet? And what about those close to him? If we find nothing in Mark's finances, what about the family? Friends? Acquaintances? It's a lot of work, I know, but his murder could have been a cover-up of fraudulent activity, and everything else, a cover-up of the murder. We are talking hundreds of thousands of pounds. Let's keep digging."

She was about to leave, but turned back. "One more thing, Mark Turner was suffering from an undiagnosed neuromuscular disorder, one whose symptoms increases with stress. Was he feeling stressed on the hike in which he first found that cave? If so, why? Could this tie in with his findings, knowledge, or suspicions concerning those frauds?"

Dai pulled a face. "People keep cuttings for many reasons, ma'am."

"I agree." She nodded. "Some people do, but we found no evidence of Turner keeping cuttings of anything else, or at any other time. He linked those cases long before Serious fraud squad did. How? Why? I am convinced he knew something. I want us to get to the bottom of it."

DEWI WATCHED the conversations unfolding around the Dolfor Moors cave. Todd Garrett had affirmed his wish to accompany John Blackman to it. Blackman wished to pay his condolences and homage to his friend and wanted to know if he could feel the same vibrations Mark had.

Pierre Gram, as expected, vehemently voiced his disdain of this, while praising the two men's hiking records.

Not for the first time, Dewi marvelled at Gram's ability to work them. Both Blackman and Garrett were fully engaged with the conversation, even encouraging it.

The sergeant had concerns about Blackman's wife and unborn baby due any day. If the birth happened later that week, the planned trip to the cave, and therefore their surveillance operation, would be off.

He was still musing on this when his phone rang. "Dewi Hughes."

"Hey, Dewi, it's Anne in Newtown Maternity."

He sat upright. "Has she had it?"

"Mrs Blackman gave birth this morning to a baby boy. Eight pounds."

"What time was this?" Dewi frowned.

"Six-thirty this morning."

"Right, thank you. Can you tell me whether the father was at the birth?"

"He was, initially, then he left to pick up some things."

"Right, thank you."

As he put the phone down, Dewi checked his watch. Noon. He had watched the conversation on social media for over an hour, and Blackman had been present for almost all of that. Some new father he was.

Dewi shrugged. Perhaps Blackman's second child was not as exciting to him as his first. Still, it seemed odd to the sergeant, himself a doting father and grandfather. But everybody was different.

CALLUM FOUND Yvonne grabbing herself a coffee. "Ma'am."

"Callum? What is it?"

"As requested, I have delved into the finances of those around Mark Turner, including Rob Tanner, from the outdoor equipment store in town."

"Go on."

"The business is his."

"What do you mean?" She frowned. "Rob Tanner owns it?"

"Yes."

"So, he is not merely the manager?"

"No. He registered the business in his name."

"Why didn't he tell me that? I asked him if he was the store manager, and he said he was. He didn't elaborate. I wonder why? Surely, the natural thing would have been for him to tell me he owns it. Most people would be proud of that fact, wouldn't they?"

"That's not the only thing, ma'am. Around three months ago, a large sum of money passed through the business account."

"How much?"

"Around fifty thousand pounds, that remains unexplained. It doesn't tally with sales records as far as I can see."

"Thanks, Callum. Speak to the DCI. Tell him we need a court order to request Rob Tanner's full accounts and records, personal and business. Let's go through it with a fine-tooth comb. Let fraud squad know, if you think there is anything untoward."

"Will do." Callum nodded. "This'll keep me busy. Enjoy your coffee." He grinned. "It's all right for some people."

She pulled her tongue out.

"Mature." He laughed.

Yvonne sipped the fiery liquid. Fifty thousand pounds was a sizeable amount of money to appear out of nowhere.

What had Rob Tanner been up to? And why hadn't he told her that he owned the store?

She didn't have to wait long for answers.

He was at the station the following day, red-faced and fists clenched, demanding to know why police had gotten a court order to go through his accounts?

"We have reason to suspect that Mark Turner's death was linked to fraud involving large sums of money. We flagged your business as one which had a sizeable sum go through it, of unexplained origin. We are going through the finances of anyone with a connection to Mark, particularly if there was tension between him and them."

His eyes narrowed.

She got the feeling he did not like her. "Why didn't you tell me you owned the business?"

He shrugged. "You asked me if I managed it. I said I did. That is true, and I was busy locking the shop to stop people coming in on us. I didn't think it was that important, or that it made any difference to anything."

"Are you prepared to answer questions now?"

He checked his watch, his face still red. "Sure, I have a short while to spare."

"Take a seat, Mr Tanner. I will grab my colleague, and we will go to an interview room."

"Why?"

"More private." Her eyes skimmed the empty waiting room. "We could have people coming in at any moment."

26

SLIPPERY SUSPECTS

T he DI found Callum hard at work at his terminal. "Can you be available for interview in about five minutes?"

"Ma'am?" He raised his eyebrows.

"Rob Tanner has just shown up. He isn't happy about us going through his accounts. He's agreed to answer questions. Is your material good to go?"

He nodded. 'I think I've got enough, yes. I'm happy to go ahead. Give me five, just to gather everything together."

"Great, I'll meet you down there. I'll take him into the interview room."

TANNER SAT with his arms folded, his expression surly.

Yvonne made a point of writing notes and questions she wanted to ask. It didn't hurt to let him stew for a few moments. Might make him more forthcoming.

He sighed repeatedly while they waited for Callum to arrive.

The DI ignored it.

Callum came in, carrying a sheaf of papers.

She cleared her throat. "Mr Tanner, I am DI Giles, and this is DC Callum Jones. We have questions regarding a sum of fifty-seven thousand pounds that went through your accounts back in February and, for which, we could find no explanation. Can you tell us what this money was about? DC Jones will show you the bank statement, if you need to jog your memory."

"I need to see it." He nodded for Callum to show the paperwork.

It appeared disingenuous to the DI. He was buying time. "Does seeing the figures help?" she asked, looking over her glasses at him.

"It does." He jerked back in his chair.

"Can you tell us where it came from? And where it went?"

He grimaced. "I really don't want to have to do this, but you are leaving me no choice." He sighed.

"Go on, Mr Tanner." Yvonne kept her gaze steady.

"Well, I told you about my partner, Helen?"

She nodded. "You did."

"Well, her father is into property. Buy-to-lets and buying houses to enhance and sell on."

"Okay..."

"He needed a favour." Tanner sighed. "My business had lost money, and he wanted to put his profit from a house sale through my business to save tax. A substantial amount of tax."

"I'm not clear." She tilted her head. "Wouldn't the sale money have been paid into his account, anyway? How could subsequently putting it through your business help him?"

"Not all the sale money went through the normal channels. The stated sale price was not the actual sale price. A third of the sale-money was cash, saving both him and the buyer money. He had some difficulty with the authorities, the year before, and so he asked me to help with this transaction. I would avoid paying tax on the money, because my business had lost sizeable sums, so I wouldn't technically owe anything to HMRC. The money was only in my account for a few weeks. It went back to him via another account. I don't know all the details."

Yvonne tapped her pen on her chin. "What made you get involved in such a scheme? If you are running a small and legitimate business, why would you risk everything to help him in his cheating?"

"Helen." He sighed. "I did it for Helen."

"Did she ask you to?"

"No, she wouldn't do that, but she worried about him. He knew they would issue him a massive underpaid tax bill, and Helen thought his business would fold, and he and her mum could lose their home."

"So, you laundered his money."

"If you want to put it that way, yes."

"You know we will check out your story? And, if he has committed a crime, we are duty-bound to report it. You know that? If there are mitigating circumstances, we can pass that along, but you wouldn't honestly expect us to cover anything up."

He shook his head.

"Thank you, Mister Tanner. We'll be in touch."

After Tanner left, Yvonne pondered whether he could be Pierre Gram. She would have asked him about his use of social media, but she did not want to spook the Grim reaper so close to their surveillance operation.

ONE SUSPECT YVONNE wanted to speak to again was Roy Joseph.

As the boyfriend of Sally Jenkins, Mark Turner's Ex-partner, and someone who had directly threatened Mark, he was still high on the suspect list, and had not satisfactorily explained where he was the day Mark was murdered.

If she was right, and someone killed Gary Sheldon to make it appear that a serial killer was on the loose, then she needed to know where Joseph was when Gary died.

First, however, she would speak with Sally, who was waiting in interview room one.

Sally cast her eyes around the walls and up at the camera in the corner, her arms stretched out in front of her, across the table, her fingers entwined.

Yvonne entered, carrying her notes and two coffees, one of which she handed to the girl.

Sally wasn't in gym clothes. She had dressed more formally, in a cream blouse and black skirt.

Yvonne wondered if that was because of attending the station. She took her seat opposite. "I know you have a busy schedule, Sally, and I appreciate you taking the time out to come and answer questions."

Sally shrugged. "I assumed I didn't have much choice?"

"You have a choice. Just as you had a choice over whether to engage a duty solicitor."

"I don't need a solicitor." Sally fixed her eyes on the DI. "Why would I?"

"Just let me know if you change your mind."

"Thanks, I will." Sally's wide eyes, and raised brows, bade Yvonne get on with it."

The DI obliged. "Sally, do you remember when you and

I last spoke, we discussed the fact that yourself and Mark Turner ran up several thousand pounds in debt?"

The girl nodded. "I remember."

"What was Mark's response to that debt?"

"I thought I told you? He took control of the finances, monitoring what was coming in and going out. I basically couldn't buy a packet of crisps without him wanting to know about it."

"Was that because he believed you responsible for the debt? Did he blame you?"

"Well, yes, he did. I bought more clothes and toiletries than he did. Though, when he spent money, it was often on bigger items, like laptops or Bluetooth earphones. He contributed a fair share to that debt. I just spent money more often. If I felt down. Comfort buying, you know."

"Were you depressed?"

"Well, we argued sometimes, and I would feel down. I would go online just to browse and end up spending money."

"I see. You should remember that no-one has a right to control your money, unless you have agreed it with them."

"Well, I agreed it with him, at first. I felt guilty, you see. Each time I spent money, I felt awful about increasing our debt. At those times, I would agree to anything."

"I see. Did you have a say in what Mark spent?"

Sally shrugged. "Not really, though he let me know when he bought something."

"Okay."

"But, because he spent money less often, I always felt I owed him at least that much."

"Right..." Yvonne scanned her notes as she approached a critical part of the interview. "Sally, were you aware of Mark keeping cuttings from newspapers, and putting them in a file?"

Sally frowned, her eyes darting to-and-fro, leading the DI to suspect she had been very aware, but was unsure how to answer. She remained silent.

"Did you see him cutting up newspapers?"

Sally chewed the inside of her cheek.

"Sally?"

"I saw him using scissors on newspapers, yes."

Was the girl obfuscating? "And what did he do with the bits he cut out? Do you remember?"

"I don't know. I think he put them in a folder, yes."

"I see. Did he talk to you about it? Tell you why he was doing it?"

Sally shook her head. "No, he didn't."

"Did you ask him why he was doing it?"

"No."

"Are you telling me you were not even slightly curious why he would cut out and keeping articles from newspapers?"

"Well, of course I wondered why he was doing it."

"But you never asked him?"

"Well, I may have asked him once." Sally sighed.

"What was his answer?"

"I can't remember."

"You can't remember?"

Sally shook her head, but averted her gaze.

"What if I told you those stories were all about cases of fraud against the elderly?"

"Fraud?" Sally's eyes widened, her mouth hanging open.

Yvonne felt the look was feigned. "Yes, Sally, fraud. Each story was about a significant amount of money. In one case, we are talking over one-hundred-thousand pounds."

Air whistled through Sally's teeth as her cheeks puffed out. "Wow!" This time, the surprise appeared genuine. "I had no idea it was that much."

"So, you knew?" Got you, Yvonne thought.

"Well, I..." Sally dropped her gaze to her hands.

"Why would Mark keep those stories, Sally? What significance were they to him?"

Sally shrugged. "Maybe, he knew the elderly people involved?"

"What, all of them?"

The girl chewed her lip. "Maybe, I don't know."

"Would be a little unusual, don't you think? Him knowing all the victims? I'm not saying he didn't, it's just that the victims came from all over Wales. Let's see, now..." Yvonne shuffled the papers in front of her. "We have Wrexham, Tredegar, Swansea, Porth Cawl, even Anglesey."

Sally grimaced.

"They cover an enormous area, don't you agree?"

"Yes, that is almost all of Wales."

"Exactly. Unless..." Yvonne studied Sally's face.

Sally looked up, wide-eyed. "What?"

"Unless you're right, and he knew all the victims."

Sally cleared her throat.

"But, if he did, might that not be because he had some involvement in what happened to them?"

"I don't know."

The DI thought she detected a tremor in Sally's voice. "Were you involved in the crimes?"

"No." Sally's eyes flashed fire. "I wasn't. Of course I wasn't. Why would I have been? How would I? I have never even stolen a packet of sweets."

"Is there anyone else you can think of, who might have

been involved? Someone Mark knew? Someone who worried him?"

Sally narrowed her eyes, her head tilted in thought. "I honestly don't know. I can have a think and get back to you." Sally checked her watch, giving off an air of having to be somewhere.

"If you like." The DI nodded, "I am happy for you to give it some thought and contact me if you have any ideas."

"Can I go now?" Sally pushed her chair back.

"One more thing." Yvonne kept her gaze steady. "Your new partner, Roy, has a police record."

"What's that got to do with it?"

"Including a previous conviction for fraud at his old place of work."

Sally appeared to shrink several inches. "What has that got to do with it?"

"Did you see Roy before you and Mark split up?"

"I don't know, I can't remember."

"Perhaps, Mark believed your boyfriend had involvement in one or more of these crimes? Could that be it?"

"That's ridiculous!" Sally stood. "What is this? Are you trying to say that either Roy or myself killed Mark because he suspected us of being involved in defrauding the elderly of colossal sums of money?"

Yvonne kept her tone even. "That's what you are saying. I didn't say that."

"Yeah well, that idea is just crazy, and you'd be wasting valuable time going down that path. You should be out there looking for Mark's killer. Who cares if he had a folder full of cuttings or six folders of them. Someone murdered him, and it wasn't Roy, and it sure-as-hell wasn't me."

"Roy made serious threats against him in the Buck Inn,

in the weeks leading up to his death. And, whether or not you agree, that places him high on our suspect list."

"We discussed that already. It was bravado after a few drinks." Sally placed her hands on her hips.

"Did you say something to Roy to make him angry at Mark because of what he saw as emotional abuse? Because Mark controlled all the money in his relationship with you? The regime that you had agreed upon with Mark because of your level of debt."

"Look, I did not want trouble that night. I told you, When I saw Mark in the pub, I tried to get Roy out of there. Roy refused. I couldn't exactly drag a grown man out of a public house, and not in front of everyone, including his friends, even if I was strong enough."

"Could Roy have had an ulterior motive for staying?"

Sally tossed her head. "You know what? I don't know. Why don't you ask him?"

"Oh, don't worry, I intend to."

ROY JOSEPH SCOWLED AT HER.

"Mr Joseph," She began. "Would you submit to a DNA test?"

His face creased, a look of disgust coddling his countenance.

The interview room was pin-drop quiet.

The DI let the silence hang there for several seconds.

Roy stretched his legs under the table, the toes of his muddy boots appeared to the right-hand side of her chair legs.

She flicked a glance at them, then back to his face.

"Well, would you?"

Arms folded, he tutted several times. He appeared to be pondering what to do. "No, you don't have a right to ask me to do any such thing, unless you are arresting me for something. And you can't do that without reasonable suspicion. I emphasise reasonable, because I have done nothing wrong, so your suspicions would not be reasonable. You're pissing in the wind."

"You seem angry, Mr Joseph." Yvonne's words were soft, but her gaze pierced him.

"I am angry. You upset my partner, virtually accuse me of fraud and, or, of murdering Mark Turner, and now you want a DNA swab. Well, I ought to give you one. Get you off my back. But do you know what? I'm not going to. If you want one, work for it. You get evidence that involves me in any crime, you can arrest me, and have your DNA. Otherwise? You can whistle."

"It would be very easy to rule you out of any involvement in Mark's death."

"I don't care."

"Fine."

"Was there anything else?"

"Well, there-"

"Oh, I knew it. Got yourself a little list, I see. If one attack doesn't succeed, you try another one. What's it this time? Throwing my toys out of the pram?"

The DI smiled despite herself. "Well, if it was, you'd be guilty as charged."

He scowled. "Very funny."

"When you argued with Mark Turner in the Buck, the night you threatened him, how did the argument start?"

"I told you before, he'd been abusing Sally in their relationship. Holding the purse strings. Not allowing her to buy anything without running it past him. The guy was a control freak. I told him that."

"That he was a control freak?"

"Yes, basically."

"So, let me get this straight, you walk up to him in the bar, and what? You tell him he's a control freak, just like that?"

"Well, no, I don't remember who spoke first. I thought he spoke to me first, but I can't be sure. Probably said something abusive."

"Your partner said she wanted you to leave fearing, if you stayed, there would be trouble. Why did you stay? Was it because you wanted to argue with him?"

"No, I wanted a drink, and I didn't see why we should be the ones to leave and go somewhere else. Why couldn't he leave?"

"You had only just arrived at the pub. He had been there a while. Am I right?"

"How is that relevant?"

"It was easier for you to leave, you didn't yet have a drink."

"Yes." he said from between gritted teeth. "But then, we come back to why should I have to be the one to go? Why couldn't we have a drink there and have no trouble?"

"Because, perhaps, you wanted to challenge him about what you saw as his abusive behaviour towards Sally. Perhaps, the idea had been eating you up, to where you wanted to do something about it. You'd had a few drinks."

"The argument was nothing." He tutted.

"Threatening to do someone in is not nothing, Mr Joseph. The law takes threats to kill seriously. If he had pressed charges, there were plenty of witnesses to guarantee a prosecution."

Joseph grunted. "He wouldn't have done that. He knew I was right, and it would have all come out in court and he wouldn't have wanted to risk that."

"What do you mean?" Yvonne leaned in. "What would all come out? What had he done?"

Joseph leaned back. "Nothing."

"Well, it's clearly not nothing. You're telling me that Mark Turner would not have prosecuted you for threats to kill, because he was afraid of what might come out in court. I would like you to explain that to me. Explain your thinking."

"Well, I just meant that, you know…"

"No, I don't know. That's why I'm asking."

"Well, the way he treated Sally."

"We've just discussed that, and even Sally agrees that she and Mark needed to save money. So, what else was there to be afraid about? Are you alluding to criminal activity? Or personal problems?"

"Forget it. I was talking through my backside. I don't know."

"You have a previous conviction for fraud, Mister Joseph."

He frowned, banging his fist down on the table. "What has that got to do with anything?"

"Mark Turner was collecting newspaper stories relating to frauds committed all over Wales. Were you aware of that?"

"No, why would I be?"

"Well, I was simply wondering if that could have been the reason for your argument?"

"What, that he suspected me of the frauds?"

"Or that you suspected him of them, yes."

"You're crazy." He blew air through his teeth.

"I'm just doing my job."

"Are you arresting me for a crime?" He pushed his chair away from the table.

The DI shook her head. "No."

"Then, I am leaving and, if you need to see me again, you can book me that duty solicitor you offered. I've had enough of your suppositions." He rose to go.

Yvonne nodded to the PC on the door for him to let Joseph out.

She remained seated for five minutes after the interview, feeling drained. She rubbed her temples in a vain attempt to fend off a developing headache. The DI was not sure she was any nearer to the heart of the case.

The DCI found her still seated in the interview room. "Are you all right, Yvonne?"

She could hear the concern in his softened voice.

"Yes, yes, I'm fine. My head is just sore." She sighed. "Is everything okay?"

He nodded. "With me? Yes, of course." He perched on the edge of the table. "I came to tell you that they have given us the go-ahead to resource the cave surveillance, chopper and all."

"Really?" Her face lit up. "That is fantastic." She narrowed her eyes. "Dogs?"

He nodded. "The complete kit and caboodle."

"I needed that. It gives us four days to get organised. Thank you, Chris."

"You're welcome." He stood. "Do you need to get off home? Rest that head?"

She shook it. "No, sir, I'll take a painkiller. I have too much to do. I can't go home now."

"Very well then, don't work too late. I want you out of here by six o'clock at the very latest."

"Yes, sir."

True to her word, Yvonne was at her car at six-ten that evening. It didn't feel right. It felt early, after having worked much later for ten days straight.

Evening birdsong filled the air, and the DI breathed deep of the late summer scent.

Showering early, and preparing herself for bed at nine, it surprised her to get a call. The DCI had said he would be the emergency contact for the case.

It was Tasha. "Hello, you."

"Tasha." Yvonne's tiredness left her. "How's it going down there?"

"Great." Tasha sounded breathless. "Unbelievably well, actually. The Met have their man!"

"Really?"

"Yes, really. They bagged him in the early hours of this morning. I should be back in time for the weekend."

"Oh, Tasha, I can't tell you how much that means to me. I needed to hear it."

"Great, I thought you would be pleased. I would have made it a surprise, but I couldn't wait to talk to you. I've been missing you like crazy."

"And I you, Tasha, you have no idea."

"Perhaps, I can take you to dinner Saturday night? I thought maybe the little Italian on Park Street-"

"Oh..." Yvonne sighed.

"What? Is something wrong?"

"I'm sorry, Tasha, normally that wouldn't be a problem, but this Saturday..."

"Look, it's all right. If you have something on, we'll do it another night."

"It's an operation, Tasha. Surveillance and capture, we're hoping."

"Ah, well then, prioritise that. I wouldn't expect anything else. We'll do it another night, okay?"

"Are you sure?"

"Of course."

"Thank you for understanding, Tasha. You are a star."

"I'll speak to you soon and see you in a couple of days."

"Brilliant. I love you."

"I love you, too."

On the other end, Tasha stared at the small velvet box clutched in her hand, wondering if fate had other ideas.

No, she determined, it was just one more delay. She'd had setbacks before. It was no biggie. She would deal with it.

27

STAKEOUT

T he morning of the stakeout arrived.

Yvonne watched as her team got their gear together, aware that uniformed units were already on scene, monitoring the covert camera feed.

An ARV unit with armed officers was also on site, along with a dog team on standby, and three personnel from South and Mid-Wales Cave Rescue Team, ready to move if something went wrong.

The DI need only get her own team on site, and into position, and guide the primary operation.

DCI Llewelyn had agreed for her to head the mission.

They knew John Blackman and Todd Garrett planned to enter the mine at eleven am. Yvonne wanted to be there by nine-thirty.

Limited cover meant reliance on the bank of trees to the left, and a hedgerow to the right, of the dip where the cave was located.

Anyone using the hedge would spend a long periods in a crouch. All part of the job, but hard on the knees and ankles.

It was Dewi's remit to check they had the equipment they needed, and that it was working. Stab vests, headsets, handsets, and freshly charged batteries. He got them all to check they could send and receive messages and that they had pepper spray, cuffs, and batons.

"Good to go?" Yvonne asked, fastening the final velcro straps on her stab vest.

They each concurred.

"Then, let's do it. Are you okay to drive, Dewi?"

"I am." He cleared his throat to hide the nerves. "Ready when you are, ma'am."

She checked her watch. "Okay, guys. This is it. It's ten-past-nine. Let's roll."

The winding drive uphill, through Dolfor, from Newtown never failed to take her breath. The landscape climbed steeply in places, the sides of the mountains encouraged the rolling mists to tumble down during spring and late autumn. Today, it was bathed in sunlight, lending an energy to the rich green tones.

Soon, they were up out of the town, having rounded the Devil's Elbow bend, and witnessed the outstanding view of the valley, and diminutive streets and houses, below.

Open skies and a varied landscape rendered the vista one of the most spectacular in Britain.

The DI smiled to herself. Moving to Wales was one of the best things she had ever done. It was hard to regret any part of the decision on a day like today.

Now, however, she had to focus. Lives depended on it. They had a killer to catch.

Within twenty minutes, they had joined the dog team amongst the trees.

A trained marksman, suited in black protective gear, had his sights trained on the cave mouth. Other members of his team were scattered among the cover and crouched behind the hedgerow.

Garrett and Blackman would park in the lay-by, a thousand yards down the hill, next to Dewi's unmarked police car. Police four-by-fours had been hidden further up.

Yvonne wasn't sure whether the killer would park in the lay-by or not, but suspected he was more likely to leave his vehicle where it wasn't immediately obvious. Perhaps he would hike part of the way.

She could feel the sweat building on her upper lip, that uncomfortable greasy feeling one gets in the heat. The stab vest and thick, tactical boots made cooling difficult. She retrieved a water bottle from her pack and took several swigs. Two hours would feel more like ten in this heat.

A black Audi approached from their left, Snaking fast around the bends, until it slowed on its approach to the lay-by.

A shout came over the radio for everyone to ready themselves.

The DI was expecting Pierre Gram to arrive first. It surprised her when more than one man exited the vehicle.

She passed the binoculars to Dewi. "There's two of them."

"Is there?" He adjusted the frames. "You're right... Hang on, I think that's Blackman and Garrett. Look." He handed the binoculars back to her. "You've seen Blackman in the flesh. I've only seen his profile photo and action pics. Is that him?"

Yvonne stared at the two men. It was Blackman and, likely, Garrett. She sighed. "Where is the Reaper?"

"Maybe he has decided to wait until after they have entered the cave." Dewi frowned.

Yvonne shook her head. "I don't like it. Something's wrong."

"Let's give it time," Her sergeant reassured. The cave's been searched. We know it's empty. We have a lot of boots on the ground, covering the situation. If the Reaper is intent on causing harm today, we'll get him"

The DI smiled. "Thanks, Dewi." She continued watching the men as they shouldered their gear and made their way towards the cave.

"Are you sure there is silver in the mine?" Garrett grabbed his bag from the boot.

"I'm sure. The Romans knew what they were doing."

"If there isn't, I'll expect cash. Thirty percent of everything we made off the last job."

"The money isn't available yet, you know that."

Garrett ran a hand through his hair. "I am sick of your excuses. We had an agreement. You wouldn't have been able to persuade them without my help."

"You'll get your money, eventually. We have to take it steady. We can't be too obvious. They'll be onto us. In the meantime, we grab the ore Mark found and we cash it in. You can have most of the take."

As Blackman and Garrett donned their helmets, elbow and knee pads, and hoisted their rucksacks on their backs, Yvonne turned the binoculars from them, to the road, and back again.

WHERE WAS PIERRE GRAM?

Scattered around, officers were becoming hot, tired, and drained, as the initial excitement evaporated. But she knew they would respond when needed.

She gave the binoculars back to Dewi.

28

THE VALUE OF THINGS

Tasha gazed around for a seat, having boarded her change at Birmingham New Street. The journey back to Newtown always felt like three steps forward, two steps back. She had one more change at Shrewsbury. There were direct trains from London, but they were at six am, and not very practical.

The carriage was hot enough to melt chocolate and airless, the only inlet being the tiny windows that were too high to have an impact. She wondered what the point of such windows was. Not only was 'Brief Encounter' made in a time romantically free of technology, but the trains had useful windows.

Around her, people were lost in their headphones, phones, and laptops. They were in the same place as she, but inhabiting other worlds entirely. She doubted that films like 'Brief Encounter' could be made today. The chances of strangers getting to know each other, or even making significant eye contact, was slim. How was romance to thrive in today's world?

She thought of Yvonne, and how lucky she felt to have

found her. The DI was unique, refusing to be a slave to the increasingly sophisticated devices on the market. Technology had its place, but Yvonne did not let it encroach on her personal life.

Tasha extracted the velvet box from her pocket, flicking it open to remind herself of the beauty of its content. She hoped Yvonne would like the diamond and sapphire ring as much as she did.

The adolescent girl opposite seemed curious about it, her blue eyes glistening.

The psychologist gave her a smile, before closing the lid and replacing the package in her pocket. The DI would see it soon enough.

HE WATCHED GARRETT GO FIRST, gazing in awe at the cavern which opened up. The cave no-one had known was there until Mark Turner discovered it.

"It feels eerie, knowing that someone died here."

He could swear he had just seen Garrett shudder. "It's large inside, don't you think?" He slipped his rucksack off his back.

"I'm amazed no-one found it before."

Remnants of police tape, and chalked markings, remained near the opening to the tunnel at the back of the chamber.

Garrett stared at it.

"Does it spook you?" Blackman moved closer, standing just behind and to the left of the younger man. Sweat beaded on his forehead.

"Yeah, it does a bit." Garrett threaded his thumbs under his shoulder straps. "Doesn't it scare you?"

Blackman shrugged. "I think Mark was unfortunate to run into a killer out here, of all places."

"You were his friend, weren't you?" Garrett turned round. "It must cut you up, coming here?"

He nodded. "It's a reminder, but Mark wouldn't have wanted us to dwell. He'd want us to explore."

Garrett nodded. "I don't feel anything. I mean, nothing in here is vibrating, or making my body shake."

"Me neither," Blackman agreed. "I guess Mark had a vivid imagination."

As Garrett moved to explore the mouth of the tunnel, Blackman waited for his opening. He had rehearsed this in his mind. One swift movement, keeping up the pressure until Garrett stopped struggling.

After it was done, he would bash his own head on the walls, bruising and bloodying himself. He'd wait half an hour, then stumble to the car and call the emergency services. If they asked why he had blood on his gloves, well, he run to his friend and tried to revive him. The cave killer got away.

Garrett paused as though having second thoughts about the tunnel. "I bet there won't be much ore in there, how could there be?"

"Mark said it was a lot."

"How was it still here after all this time?"

"No-one's been in here since the Romans. Soil and rockfall covered the entrance. If it wasn't for the extreme weather we have had recently, it would still be hidden."

"Is that why they killed mark? Because they knew he'd found something?"

Blackman tilted his head. "Maybe, his death wasn't random. Perhaps someone else was after that ore."

"But who?" Garrett's body stiffened as the blood drained from his face. "The only person who knew about it was you. He found out, didn't he? He found out about the frauds. You never intended paying me. You killed him."

29

A KILLER UNMASKED

Yvonne frowned, pacing. The same niggling doubts clawed at her.

Blackman's readiness to go caving so close to his child being born, and after his best friend was killed, didn't sit right. People dealt with grief in unique ways, she knew that, but Blackman had expressed a fear for his wife and child and still gone exploring. His dichotomy bothered her.

"What changed?" She mused aloud.

"Sorry?" Dewi passed her the binoculars.

"I was wondering what changed to make Blackman so ready to visit this cave after telling me he wouldn't."

"He said he wanted to pay homage, didn't he?"

"Sure, but I warned him, Dewi. I warned him against coming here. Why would he risk coming here with a killer on the loose?"

"And Gram made a comment about the baby being due. That should have woken him up to the risks, shouldn't it?" her sergeant agreed.

She ran a hand through her hair; the frown having deepened.

"Yvonne?" Dewi put a hand on her arm.

"How did he know?"

"How did who know what?"

"How did Gram know that Blackman was expecting a baby? I saw nothing in those transcripts about a baby."

Dewi rubbed his chin. "I didn't see it mentioned either."

"Do you think Gram knows Blackman, personally? Mark Turner had that folder of fraud stories. That had to have meant something to him, otherwise he wouldn't have gone to the trouble to cut and keep. We've been all over his accounts and he sure as hell did not have any money. He was still in debt when he died."

"True."

"So, why keep them? If he had suspicions, why didn't he come to us?"

"Maybe he wasn't sure?"

"Or maybe he cared about the person he thought responsible."

"The ex-girlfriend?" Dewi offered. "She would know Blackman was having a baby."

"Well, the perp is male, so would have to be her recent boyfriend in that case. But I don't think so. They still have debt. No, the person Mark cared most about was Blackman."

"You think-"

"Yes." She nodded. "I think Pierre Gram is Blackman, and he's in there with someone else whose life may be in danger. We have to go in."

She cranked the handset. "I think the killer is in the cave. We need to go, go, go!"

The scene changed from one of quiet surveillance, to

controlled activity, as armed officers moved with stealth to the cave mouth, weapons raised.

"IT's YOU." Todd Garrett took a step back. "What did you do? Did you follow him here? Were you waiting for him?"

Blackman stepped forward, the garrotte gripped in the hand in his right jacket pocket.

"Why did you kill him?" Garrett took another pace back. "There's no silver, is there?"

"Oh, the penny's finally dropping." Blackman sneered, his knuckles white where he held the Garrotte. He reached for Garrett as the latter made a run for it. He stretched out a foot, bringing the younger man down, and jumping on him, his knee in Garrett's back so he could not get up. Blackman slid the garrotte over the young man's head in one swift movement.

"No. No, please, John," Garrett pleaded.

"Armed police! Put down your weapon!"

Garrett blinked at the flashlights in his face, beyond which it was impossible to see.

"Armed police! Drop your weapon or we will shoot," the officers called again.

There was a moment.

The police held their breath.

Blackman dropped the Garrotte and raised his hands, holding his forearm over his eyes to protect them from the harsh light.

His victim rasped for breath, coughing and spluttering, while his airways returned to normal, nursing a flesh wound created as the wire dug in.

They cuffed Blackman to the back and dragged him

outside, where Yvonne had the privilege of cautioning him, and arresting him on suspicion of murder and attempted murder.

They would take a DNA swab back at the station, but the DI felt sure she had her man.

PROPOSAL

L a Traviatta, the Italian restaurant on Park Street, was full. Tasha felt lucky to have gotten them in with her booking the night before.

She wore a smart white shirt and pant suit; the feminine cut hugging her slender figure.

Yvonne wore a red dress with small gold flowers, after Tasha had warned she would need to dress up.

The waiting staff buzzed around the tables, making sure the guests had drinks and were happy with their food, and the manager, himself, came to their table to take the orders.

After they ordered their antipasto starters, Yvonne sat back in her chair, staring at her partner. "You look amazing, Tasha, your eyes are glowing. I can tell you caught your man in London."

Tasha grinned. "You're looking pretty fine yourself, DI Giles, and I hear you also got your man. As though the outcome was ever in doubt."

Yvonne shook her head. "Oh, there were many moments of doubt, and it all came very close to going pear-shaped at the end. I almost missed a glaringly obvious clue."

Tasha laughed. "That wouldn't have had anything to do with missing me, would it? A little preoccupied, were you?"

"Ha Ha." Yvonne grinned despite herself. "I missed you, and you occupied far too much of my brain power."

"I'm sorry." Tasha leaned over. "I really didn't want to go."

The DI smiled. "It's fine... I'm teasing you."

"I know. It was still bad timing."

Yvonne raised her brows. "Bad timing? What do you mean?"

The psychologist gave a nod to the waiter in the doorway. He headed for the kitchen.

"Tasha?"

"We need to go out back for a moment." Tasha reached over and took her hand. "Let's go."

She led the DI to the back garden of the restaurant. They had lined the pavement on either side with tealight candles in jars and scattered more of them around the garden. Coloured lights adorned the trees and pergola. The deputy manager, a man in his forties, came out clutching a mandolin, and began playing.

Yvonne looked about her in awe. "Wow, Tasha, this is beautiful."

The waiter, to whom Tasha had nodded, brought out a magnum of champagne in a bucket of ice and two chilled glasses.

The DI narrowed her eyes at her partner. "Okay, what are you up to?"

Tasha pulled out the small velvet box, her sparkling eyes fixed on Yvonne's sceptical ones. She went down on one knee, as the mandolin struck up an old Italian love song.

"Yvonne Giles, I love you more than I have ever loved. Will you do me the honour of becoming my wife?"

The End.

AFTERWORD

If you enjoyed this book, I'd be very grateful if you'd post a short review on Amazon. Your support really does make a difference and helps bring my books to more readers like you.

Mailing list: You can join my emailing list here : AnnamarieMorgan.com

Facebook page: AnnamarieMorganAuthor

You might also like to read the other books in the series:

Book 1: Death Master:

After months of mental and physical therapy, Yvonne Giles, an Oxford DI, is back at work and that's just how she likes it. So when she's asked to hunt the serial killer responsible for taking apart young women, the DI jumps at the chance but hides the fact she is suffering debilitating flashbacks. She is told to work with Tasha Phillips, an in-her-face, criminal psychologist. The DI is not enamoured with the idea. Tasha has a lot to prove. Yvonne has a lot to get over. A tentative link with a 20 year-old cold case brings them closer to the truth but events then take a horrifyingly personal turn.

Book 2: You Will Die

After apprehending an Oxford Serial Killer, and almost losing her life in the process, DI Yvonne Giles has left England for a quieter life in rural Wales.Her peace is shattered when she is asked to hunt a priest-killing psychopath, who taunts the police with messages inscribed on the corpses.Yvonne requests the help of Dr. Tasha Phillips, a psychologist and friend, to aid in the hunt. But the killer is one step ahead and the ultimatum, he sets them, could leave everyone devastated.

Book 3: Total Wipeout

A whole family is wiped out with a shotgun. At first glance, it's an open-and-shut case. The dad did it, then killed himself. The deaths follow at least two similar family wipeouts – attributed to the financial crash.

So why doesn't that sit right with Detective Inspector Yvonne Giles? And why has a rape occurred in the area, in the weeks preceding each family's demise? Her seniors do not believe there are questions to answer. DI Giles must therefore risk everything, in a high-stakes investigation ofa mysterious masonic ring and players in high finance.

Can she find the answers, before the next innocent family is wiped out?

Book 4: Deep Cut

In a tiny hamlet in North Wales, a female recruit is murdered whilst on Christmas home leave. Detective Inspector Yvonne Giles is asked to cut short her own leave, to investigate. Why was the young soldier killed? And is her death related to several alleged suicides at her army base? DI Giles this it is, and that someone powerful has a dark secret they will do anything to hide.

Book 5: The Pusher

Young men are turning up dead on the banks of the River Severn. Some of them have been missing for days or even weeks. The only thing the police can be sure of, is that the men have drowned. Rumours abound that a mythical serial killer has turned his attention from the Manchester canal to the waterways of Mid-Wales. And now one of CID's own is missing. A brand new recruit with everything to live for. DI Giles must find him before it's too late.

Book 6: Gone

Children are going missing. They are not heard from again until sinister requests for cryptocurrency go viral. The public must pay or the children die. For lead detective Yvonne Giles, the case is complicated enough. And then the unthinkable happens...

Book 7: Bone Dancer

A serial killer is murdering women, threading their bones back together, and leaving them for police to find. Detective Inspector Yvonne Giles must find him before more innocent victims die. Problem is, the killer wants her and will do anything he can to get her. Unaware that she, herself, is is a target, DI Giles risks everything to catch him.

Book 8: Blood Lost

A young man comes home to find his whole family missing. Half-eaten breakfasts and blood spatter on the lounge wall are the only clues to what happened...

Book 9: Angel of Death

He is watching. Biding his time. Preparing himself for a torturous kill. Soaring above; lord of all. His journey, direct through the lives of the unsuspecting.

The Angel of Death is nigh.

The peace of the Mid-Wales countryside is shattered, when a female eco-warrior is found crucified in a public wood. At first, it would appear a simple case of finding which of the woman's enemies had had her killed. But DI Yvonne Giles has no idea how bad things are going to get. As the body count rises, she will need all of her instincts, and the skills of those closest to her, to stop the murderous rampage of the Angel of Death.

Book 10: Death in the Air

Several fatal air collisions have occurred within a few months in rural Wales. According to the local Air Accidents Investigation Branch (AAIB) inspector, it's a coincidence. Clusters happen. Except, this cluster is different. DI Yvonne Giles suspects it when she hears some of the witness statements but, when an AAIB inspector is found dead under a bridge, she knows it.

Something is way off. Yvonne is determined to get to the bottom of the mystery, but exactly how far down the treacherous rabbit hole is she prepared to go?

Book 11: Death in the Mist

The morning after a viscous sea-mist covers the seaside town of Aberystwyth, a young student lies brutalised within one hundred yards of the castle ruins.

DI Yvonne Giles' reputation precedes her. Having successfully captured more serial killers than some detectives have caught colds, she is seconded to head the murder investigation team, and hunt down the young woman's killer.

What she doesn't know, is this is only the beginning...

Book 12: Death under Hypnosis

When the secretive and mysterious Sheila Winters approaches Yvonne Giles and tells her that she murdered someone thirty years before, she has the DI's immediate attention.

Things get even more strange when Sheila states:

She doesn't know who.

She doesn't know where.

She doesn't know why.

Book 13: Fatal Turn

A seasoned hiker goes missing from the Dolfor Moors after recording a social media video describing a narrow cave he intends to explore. A tragic accident? Nothing to see here, until a team of cavers disappear on a coastal potholing expedition, setting off a string of events that has DI Giles tearing her hair out. What, or who is the thread that ties this series of disappearances together?

A serial killer, thriller murder-mystery set in Wales.

Book 14: The Edinburgh Murders

A newly retired detective from the Met is murdered in a murky alley in Edinburgh, a sinister calling card left with the body.

The dead man had been a close friend of psychologist Tasha Phillips, giving her her first gig with the Met decades before.

Tasha begs DI Yvonne Giles to aid the Scottish police in solving the case.

In unfamiliar territory, and with a ruthless killer haunting the streets, the DI plunges herself into one of the darkest, most terrifying cases of her career. Who exactly is The Poet?

Remember to watch out for Book 15, coming soon...

Printed in Great Britain
by Amazon